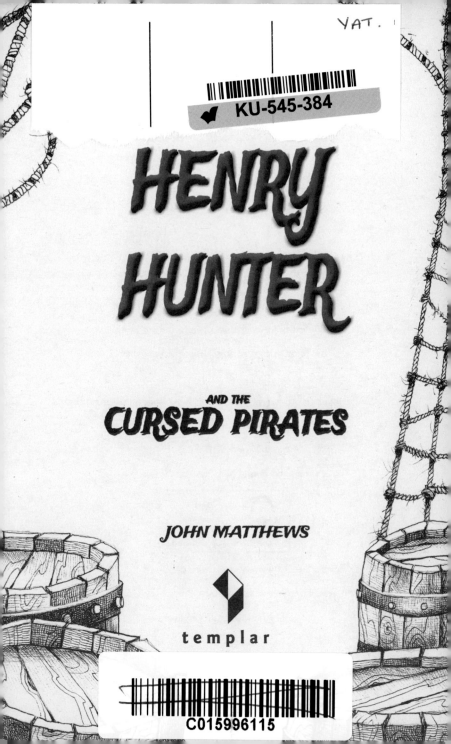

HENRY HUNTER

AND THE CURSED PIRATES

JOHN MATTHEWS

templar

First published in Great Britain in 2015

by Templar Publishing

Northburgh House, 10 Northburgh Street, London EC1V 0AT

Text copyright © John Matthews 2015

Illustrations copyright © Nick Tankard 2015

A CIP catalogue record for this book is available from the British Library.

ISBN: 978–1–783–70137–7

1 3 5 7 9 10 8 6 4 2

Printed and bound by Clays Ltd, St Ives plc

www.templarco.co.uk

Templar is part of the Bonnier Publishing Group

www.bonnierpublishing.com

To my old shipmate Ian Jackson,
who regularly sails the seven seas.
Well, almost.

A Note To All Our Faithful Readers

Just in case you haven't read the first volume of the Henry Hunter Files – *Henry Hunter and the Beast of Snagov* – I'd better explain that my friend HH is a normal boy who just happens to be incredibly smart. Henry is the son of Steven and Hortense Hunter, who invented a new kind of interactive computer chip and made so much money out of it they decided to use their millions responsibly and go off in search of a rare orchid that is rumoured to be the cure for half of the known diseases in the world. Before they left, Mr and Mrs

Hunter made Henry's two uncles, who are both millionaires, his official guardians, so that even if they don't get home very often, they know their son is well looked after. They also installed him in an old-fashioned school called St Grimbold's, where HH has his own set of rooms and only rarely attends classes because he's actually smarter than the teachers! Because his family is massively rich, he has enough money to indulge his favourite activity – hunting for strange and weird things. I met HH at St Grimbold's, where we became friends. Since then we've had many adventures in some of the most amazing places in the world. Some of them I still can't talk about, either because they are just too frightening or because they are too sensitive to be told. But this is a story from Henry's secret files that I can share. In fact I need to tell this story, because I need your help...

Adolphus Pringle

A CALL FOR HELP

"Listen to this, Dolf," said Henry Hunter. Reluctantly I tore myself away from *Deathdealers 4: the Horde*, which had been taking all my attention for the past hour. It was sports day at St Grimbold's School for Extraordinary Boys and, since neither Henry nor I much cared for three-legged races or the ten-metre dash, we were both hiding out in Henry's rooms.

I was surprised to see that HH wasn't about to quote me something from a book. Instead, he was holding a sheet of very thin paper, on which was written several lines in rather shaky-looking handwriting. Thinking that only Henry could know people who still wrote letters rather than sent emails, I gave him my full attention.

Once he was sure he had captured my interest, he began reading.

Dear Henry,

I'm writing to you because you are the only person I can think of who might be able to help me. Both my parents have disappeared, and my cousin Jack has told me to give up hope that I'll ever see them again!

But I'm sure they are somewhere out there, on the ocean, and I'm certain it's got something to do with what I saw when I was on *The Spinnaker* with them. I'm sure there was a ghost ship out on the ocean. If you think you can help, please come to the old place next Friday.

Charlie

"Sounds a bit mad to me," I said. "Who is Charlie anyway? And what's a... spinnaker?"

"Charlie Stevens is an old friend," answered Henry. "His parents knew mine before we were even born. And it sounds like the *Spinnaker* is a boat, from the way Charlie writes about it. His parents were always talking about sailing off somewhere in search of buried treasure and stuff."

"Buried treasure!"

"Well, Timothy – that's Charlie's dad – fancied himself an expert on pirates. He once told me he knew where Captain Morgan had hidden his loot."

"Who?" I asked.

"Captain Morgan was one of the greatest privateers of all time," said Henry. "He started out as a pirate and ended up as the governor of Jamaica. Then he either lost or hid all his money and lived out his last days telling stories in return for jugs of ale."

I raised my eyebrows. Captain Morgan sounded like quite a character. "What's a privateer?"

"A kind of licensed pirate," said Henry. "Kings and queens used to give a letter of marque – that's like a licence – to unscrupulous captains to go off and raid enemy ships. Then they'd bring back all sorts of treasure to fill the royal coffers."

As usual Henry was going into way too much detail, and I wasn't sure of his point. "So what does all of this have to do with your friend Charlie?"

"No idea," said Henry, smiling. "But I plan to find out."

We didn't have to wait long. That afternoon, a car arrived to pick us up and drive us into the wilds of the country. Having two millionaire uncles as guardians meant that Henry could call up a car – or even a private jet – at a moment's notice.

We drove from St Grim's in Sussex into deepest Oxfordshire, to the small town of Thame. There, we took a wandering single-track lane that wound away from the main road and ended up at a pair of big iron gates. A small camera mounted on a gatepost swivelled down to look at us, and moments later the gates swung silently open. We proceeded up a tree-lined drive to a big crumbling house with long, narrow windows. To one side of the solid wooden front door stood a huge statue of a raven carved out of smooth dark stone. On the other side was an even bigger and weirder creature that Henry explained was a griffin – half eagle and half lion. To be honest I found both statues a bit creepy, but Henry said they were carved by a famous sculptor. I wondered if that was meant to make me feel better about them. It didn't.

As we came up to the door, two huge Irish wolfhounds came bounding towards us. I know a bit about dogs from my aunt, who used to keep a poodle, but this was something else entirely. As the car stopped they stuck their faces up against the windows and barked. I flinched, thinking I'd rather be in a three-legged race at St Grim's than chewed up by one of these things – they were easily a metre tall and looked pretty fierce. But as Henry calmly opened the door they suddenly became extremely friendly and began giving him a good licking.

When I got out gingerly behind him, they repeated this kindness for me (on the whole

I preferred the time I had to take a bath in a rusty wheelbarrow, but that's another adventure...)

"Can you wait?" Henry asked the driver. "If you go around to the side of the house you'll be able to get a cup of tea from the staff." (Yes, I know, 'staff'. I told you Henry knows some pretty posh people.)

The driver nodded and we approached the big front door. Henry rang the bell – it was the old-fashioned kind where you pull a rusty handle and can just hear as it rings somewhere in the depths of the house.

It was several minutes before the door opened. Facing us was a tall, heavy-browed man with a big moustache. He glared at us.

"Well. What do you want?" he demanded.

Henry flashed him his best smile. "It's Henry Hunter, Mr Bligh. This is my friend, Adolphus Pringle. We've come to see Charlie."

"What? Oh, yes, Hunter…" said the man, frowning.

"We were sorry to hear about Mr and Mrs Stevens," said Henry.

The man's face softened a bit. "Yes. Bad business. Charles is still very upset. I'm not sure he wants to see anyone."

"I'm sure we can cheer him up," Henry

answered. "Better than just moping about, don't you think?"

"I suppose you'd better come in then," the man said. "He's upstairs in his room, I imagine."

Henry nodded and I followed him in. The house was even more impressive inside. The hall was huge with lots of old paintings hung on the walls of men and women who looked as if they had been forced to stand still too long. (One of the portraits even included two big dogs that looked a lot like the wolfhounds.) A long, curving flight of stairs led upwards to a landing off which several doors could be seen.

Henry made his way straight up the stairs to one of the doors and knocked.

It literally flew open and a tall, gangly boy with a shock of curly red hair and an enormous number of freckles grabbed Henry by the arm and pulled him inside. As I followed he stared at me suspiciously.

"This is Dolf," said Henry. "You can trust him."

"You didn't say anything to Jack?" Charlie asked anxiously. I deduced that the sour-faced man downstairs was Charlie's uncle.

"Not a word," answered Henry.

Charlie's room was large and airy, with a big window. I didn't need to be a genius like HH to work out what he was interested in. On every surface, including the floor, were model boats. Some were the small kind you can sail on ponds; others were large and graceful and looked like they should be in a museum. Most of them were old-fashioned – galleons, Henry told me later – with sails and ropes and masts sticking out everywhere. On the wall hung

a photograph of a very modern, white, sleek boat, like the something from a James Bond film. '*Spinnaker*' was painted on the side in big black letters, and on the deck stood three people – Charlie, easily identifiable by his wild red hair, and two adults who I guessed were his parents. They all looked happy and carefree.

This must the boat from which Charlie thought he had seen a ghost ship.

Henry examined the photo for a moment. Then he turned to Charlie. "So, tell us what happened."

Charlie sat down on the bed and stared at us glumly. "I'm not sure where to begin," he said slowly.

"Beginning at the beginning always works for me," grinned Henry, pulling up a spindly-looking chair and dropping into it. I hunkered down on the wooden floor and found a rather squashed but perfectly edible bar of chocolate in my jacket pocket. Together we listened to Charlie Stevens' strange and scary tale.

THE GHOST SHIP

"It was supposed to be a dream cruise," Charlie began. "My parents had always wanted to go to the Caribbean – especially my dad. You remember how he loves everything about pirates, HH? I think he's watched all the *Pirates of the Caribbean* films about a hundred times. Then this guy who owns his own yacht offered to take us all on a trip around the Caribbean and he was pretty psyched. Started planning it right away."

"Who was the guy with the boat?" asked Henry.

"Nathan Trueblood," Charlie replied. "My dad met him though business and they were mates in no time. He would come here and they'd hang out for hours, looking at charts and talking about seventeenth-century pirates. To be honest, I didn't like him much. One of those people who ruffle your hair and call you 'old chap'."

"So when did you leave on the cruise?" asked Henry.

"Last June," replied Charlie. "We flew to the US, to Florida where Nathan's yacht was moored at Key West. Then we headed down towards the Bahamas."

I wondered when he was going to get to the point of the story, but decided not to say anything and took another bite of my chocolate bar.

"When we got there everything was great. The boat was fantastic. Talk about luxurious! The weather was perfect – the sun shone all day every day and the sky and sea just seemed to get bluer. My dad wanted to stop at as many of the major pirate landmarks as possible, like Port Royal and Nassau. Port Royal was a bit of a disappointment. There was an earthquake there in—"

"1692," put in Henry. (I wasn't surprised.) "It destroyed the place and it was no longer a pirate haven. Most of them moved off to Tortuga, further along the US coast."

"Yeah," said Charlie quickly, apparently just as keen as me to avoid HH launching into a lecture. "Anyway, Dad got into a bit of an argument with some bloke he met on the docks.

Apparently they disagreed about some local legend," he added vaguely.

"Any idea what the legend was?" Henry asked.

Charlie shook his head. "Something to do with treasure, I think, but I can't remember whose."

"Never mind," said Henry. "Go on."

"Well, we left Port Royal on the fifth of July, heading for Nassau in the Bahamas. We'd been at sea for about a day and dusk was falling. We dropped anchor and my parents sat on the deck 'taking the night air', as my mum calls it. I was up on the bridge asking Captain Trueblood questions about the engines – that's what Nathan said we should call him when we were on board – when I glanced out of the window. There was a lot of mist over the water, but I was sure that I saw it!"

"What?" said Henry and I in unison.

"The ship," said Charlie.

"What ship?" There we were again, a regular duo.

"The ghost ship."

"Ghost ship?" said Henry, his eyes gleaming. "The one you mentioned in your letter?"

Charlie nodded. "I told Captain Trueblood I'd spotted something – without telling him what, in case he thought I was crazy. But he looked and said he couldn't see anything. So I went out on deck with a pair of binoculars."

Charlie stared uneasily at us and shifted on the bed. He chewed his lip, not speaking for several seconds. Then he went on with his story.

"OK. This is going to sound mad but... well, when I looked through the binoculars I couldn't see anything at all. Just mist floating on the sea. But when I looked *without* them I could definitely see a ship."

"What did it look like?" demanded Henry, leaning forward eagerly.

"There were masts and sails and stuff like that – it was like a really old-fashioned ship, the kind they have in pirate films. It was even flying a flag with a skull and crossbones! I thought it must be one of those cheesy replica ships they use for cruises. You know, 'Be a Pirate and Sail the Seven Seas' – that kind of thing. Then I noticed the ship seemed to have a greenish glow around it, and it was full of holes, as if it had been hit by loads of cannonballs, although somehow they hadn't sunk it."

Charlie stared at us with big round eyes. "The third thing I noticed was that it was headed straight for us... and it was moving far too quickly for an ordinary sailing ship..."

"Stop there for a minute," Henry said.

"Let's just recap. You say that through the binoculars there was no ship visible, yet when you looked with your naked eyes you could see it and it was glowing and had holes?"

Charlie nodded and I noticed his hands were trembling in his lap. I thought he looked about as scared as I'd ever seen anyone look. I ate the last mouthful of my chocolate as Henry asked: "OK. So what happened next?"

"That's the worst part," said Charlie. "I don't know!"

"What do you mean?"

"Well, all I can remember is that the ship got bigger and bigger, and that the nearer it got the weirder and nastier it looked. I tried to shout a warning to Captain Trueblood and my parents, but I couldn't speak. I thought I could see... people...weird, ghostly people...

on deck. Then this kind of... misty tentacle thing reached out for me. It seemed to come from the ghost ship, and I wanted to dodge it. But I was rooted to the spot and it curled round me, all cold and clammy, and I suddenly felt sick. Then I must have passed out or something."

Charlie stared at us miserably. Neither Henry nor I said anything. My mind was filled with images of the ghostly ship with its mystical crew and tentacles of mist. Henry was staring into the distance. I guessed he was thinking deeply the way only Henry can.

Eventually he looked right at Charlie and said: "What happened when you woke up?"

Charlie opened and closed his mouth a few times, then took a deep breath and carried on.

"I still felt a bit funny – dizzy, I guess – but I staggered back to the cabin. Captain Trueblood was slumped over the wheel, out cold. I could see he was still breathing, so I went to find my parents..." Charlie gulped.

"But they weren't there. I searched every centimetre of the ship – I couldn't find any sign of them. It was like they'd never been there."

Charlie's eyes brimmed with tears and he blew his nose on a handkerchief. Henry kept quiet for once and waited patiently, fiddling with a loose button on his shirt. I wished I had another chocolate bar hidden away.

Charlie blinked a few times and continued. "I managed to raise Captain Trueblood and he got the rest of the crew moving. We all searched the *Spinnaker* from end to end. There was no sign of my parents. Not a trace."

Charlie jumped up and started pacing around the room. Henry was silent but I could tell he was thinking.

"That was almost six months ago," said Charlie finally. "No one has seen or heard anything from them since. My cousin Jack came to stay while stuff was being sorted out. He says he's my legal guardian now and I should stop expecting to hear from my parents. Everyone thinks they were washed overboard by some kind of freak wave and that they're gone forever. No one believes me about the ghost ship. No one! *But I don't believe them!*"

I jumped at Charlie's sudden, loud shout – even Henry flinched.

"I know I saw that weird ship," Charlie kept on, "and I'm sure it has something to do with their disappearance."

He stopped and I realised he was looking at my raised eyebrows – I was making it much too obvious that I found all this very hard to believe.

Charlie glared at me and unbuttoned the top of his shirt, baring his left shoulder. "If you don't believe me, what's this then?" he demanded.

A large raised red welt cut across his shoulder – the kind of mark you might get if an octopus grabbed you. (I'd seen something like it on TV.)

Henry didn't look too closely at the welt but patted Charlie on his other shoulder in a business-like kind of way. "I think you're right, old chap."

Charlie's face lit up. "You believe me? I knew if anyone would it would be you, HH. So will you help?"

I'd already realised this was about to become our next adventure. On the face of it, Charlie's story made no sense at all, unless you believed in ghosts, which I for one did not – not then, anyway. And what about that weird tentacle thing he'd mentioned? Was there some kind of monster on the ghostly ship – assuming the ship existed at all? I was already thinking about how nasty all that could turn out to be, and how dangerous, but I could see that Charlie was desperate, and Henry had that determined look that said he was about to go hunting for something, and that it was probably going to involve pirates, ghostly or not. And quite possibly treasure as well.

Henry stood up and walked over to the photo of the *Spinnaker*.

"Where's the yacht now?" he asked.

"I think Mr Trueblood said he was going to dock her in the harbour at Nassau."

"Then we need to go down there and take a look around," said Henry.

Charlie jumped up from his bed. "Can I come?" he asked, his eyes alight.

"Well, I guess you'll have to ask Jack," Henry said.

Charlie's face fell. "He'll never say yes. He thinks I have 'an overactive imagination'— that I made up what I saw because I was so upset. But I didn't, I swear!"

"We believe you, don't we, Dolf?" said Henry.

I nodded. Privately I wasn't at all sure, but it was clear that Charlie Stevens needed to hear that we believed his story. Six months is a long time to keep faith. Without friends it must have been almost impossible.

Henry stood up and flicked back his floppy hair. "We'll find your parents, Charlie," he said seriously.

Charlie managed a small smile. "Thank you. You're my last hope."

"Let's go and talk to Cousin Jack," Henry said, winking at me. "You stay here, Charlie, and I'll see if I can persuade him to let you come along."

TALES OF
HAUNTED SEAS

Cousin Jack made it clear he wasn't going to let Charlie go anywhere – especially not with us and especially not to the Caribbean. When Henry told him that he intended to go and look for Mr and Mrs Stevens I thought Jack was literally going to explode.

"I've never heard of anything so ridiculous," he said. "Just because your guardians give you more licence than is good for you, Hunter, doesn't mean I'm going to do the same with

Charles. In the first place you won't find anything, because there's nothing to find. And in the second I don't want all this raked up again. Charles has been through enough and I have told him that he has to accept the fact that his parents are gone for good. The last thing he needs is to go gallivanting around the Caribbean in search of some imaginary ship!"

Henry was far too wise to argue. He just smiled his toothy grin and shook Mr Bligh's hand. "I expect you're right, sir," he said politely.

Now I know that when Henry Hunter smiles like that, and calls an adult 'sir' it means he's already planning to do exactly what he likes, regardless of their opinion; but Charlie's Cousin Jack didn't know him as well as me. He huffed and puffed a bit and muttered things like: "I should think so too." Then he suddenly seemed to relent.

"Look, lads," he said, not shouting this time. "All I want is what's best for Charles. As long as he's here with me I know he's safe. It takes time to get over this kind of thing and I don't want him to get his hopes up for nothing."

"We understand, don't we, Dolf?" said Henry in his most serious voice. "If it's OK with you, sir, I'll just go and say goodbye to Charlie, then we'll be on our way and leave you in peace."

Henry slipped away for a few moments, leaving me staring uncomfortably at Mr Bligh's shoes.

When HH returned, Cousin Jack ushered us out to the car. As we were getting in he put a hand on Henry's shoulder. "I only want what's best for Charles," he said again. "If you want to visit again sometime I'm sure it will help."

As we drove away from the house I looked

back and saw Charlie standing forlornly at one of the windows. He half-raised a hand to wave at us – then seemed to forget and let it fall to his side again.

"Er... what did you tell Charlie?" I asked.

"That we're going to find out what happened to his parents," answered Henry. He looked about as serious as I'd ever seen him; then he turned and grinned at me. "Pack for warmer shores, Dolf. We're off to the Caribbean! And the best thing is we're going to find out a lot about pirates on the way... "

The flight from London Heathrow to the Bahamas was a long one, and during that time Henry made sure that it was *me* who found out a lot about pirates. Though, after raiding the Hunter Learjet's seriously well-stocked kitchen (chocolate éclairs and lemon tarts, if I remember right), I struggled to keep awake in my comfortable seat as Henry shared

'a few facts' about pirates.

"Pirates weren't jolly buccaneers like most people think," said Henry, waving a book containing lots of colour pictures of salty sea-dogs with roguish gleams in their eyes and a fair scattering of peg-legs and parrots. "They were lowlife scum of the earth – they preyed on the weak and stole everything they could to get rich and drunk on rum every day—"

"They sound like a great bunch," I put in.

"There were some good things about them. Not all of them were cruel villains – they had laws on board their ships, which were a bit like floating countries, each with their own rules, strictly dividing up the spoils, giving payments to men who got wounded in battle, and so on." Henry leaned forward and jabbed a finger at me. "Did you know, Dolf, they would get different payments for the loss of an eye, a finger, a leg or an arm?"

I shook my head, wondering if any of them hurt themselves in order to make a quid or two.

"Believe me there were plenty of opportunities to get injured," continued Henry, as if he'd read my mind. "Apart from having to survive the terrible conditions on board – no fresh food, no way to get clean, and as for the toilets…" He shuddered. "It was likely they'd get hit by a flying cannonball, or spiked with splinters when one hit the side of the ship. Those could finish you off pretty nastily."

"So most pirates were a bunch of smelly, unwashed killers, who couldn't expect to live very long?" I said.

"Their life expectancy was anything up to

six months, but sometimes a lot less. It's safe to say most of them ended up in Davy Jones's Locker."

"Davy who's what now?" I enquired, baffled.

"Davy Jones. No one is really sure who he was. Some say he was a real sailor who drowned and became a kind of sea demon. Whatever the truth, pirates used his name for the place you went if you died at sea."

"So when were these pirates around?"

It turned out to be the worst question I could have asked. It set Henry off talking about what he called the 'Golden Age of Piracy', from the middle of the seventeenth century to the middle of the eighteenth century, and how after that there was such a big push to stamp out pirates that their numbers dwindled until they'd finally all but died off.

By this point I couldn't keep my eyes open.

"But you know," Henry said, as I felt myself drifting off, "there are still pirates today. You must have seen in the news those rich people's yachts that get captured and their owners held to ransom."

That woke me up a bit.

"Do you think that's what happened to Charlie's parents?"

"It's the most obvious answer. But I'm not sure how it could tie in with what Charlie saw."

"You mean the ghost ship?"

"Yes," said Henry. "There are plenty of stories about pirate ghosts... some of them could easily be true..."

"Ghosts! You mean you believe in them now?"

"It's not that I actually believe," said

Henry. "But until I see one, I can't say I don't. After all, we didn't always know that vampires existed, did we – until we met Bella Dracul?"

He was right – as usual.

Henry pulled out a large leather-bound book from the stack he'd brought along. It had a long title – something like *Ghostly Pirates and Apparitions on the Barbary Coast*.

"There are loads of different stories," Henry said. "Ghostly pirates who come ashore in search of treasure they buried while they were alive, or who're guarding their hoard from the living. There's a bunch that are supposed to be the ghostly crew commanded by Captain Kidd, one of the most infamous pirates. It's said he buried loads of his treasure before the law caught up with him, and people have been looking for it ever since. But every now and then the ghosts of his crew come ashore and chase would-be treasure-hunters away."

I digested this for a minute or two. "So you're saying that what Charlie saw was real and that it *was* ghosts that took his parents?"

"I'm just saying it could be," answered Henry cheerfully. "That explanation's a lot more fun than modern pirates."

I wasn't sure I'd call either option fun. I rolled my eyes and asked, "So how do we start looking for them? I mean, the Caribbean isn't exactly small."

Henry looked thoughtful. "To be honest, Dolf, I'm not sure. I guess we'll start with this Captain Nathan Trueblood and the *Spinnaker* and see where that takes us."

ABOARD
THE SPINNAKER

We landed at Grantley Adams International Airport on the island of Barbados and were met at the terminal by a driver Henry had arranged, a tall Rastafarian named George Peacock, who wore super-long dreads in his hair and a permanently cheerful expression. He drove us to our glass-fronted, posh-looking hotel in Bridgetown and left us to unpack. HH and I had adjoining rooms and after I had spent the first half-hour eating the free chocolate chip cookies, checking out the TV stations and trying out a shoot-'em-up on the online games console I knocked on Henry's door.

I wasn't really surprised to find that he hadn't even started to unpack, but was sitting in the middle of the room surrounded by books and sea-charts.

"There you are, Dolf," he said absently. "George got us these. I've been mugging up on the history of the place and working out the course the *Spinnaker* took on the day Charlie's parents disappeared."

He pointed to a large chart spread out on the carpet. It was covered in pencil lines – the course of the *Spinnaker*, I guessed.

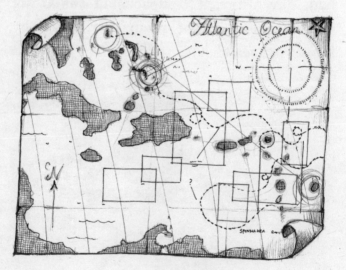

"This," he nodded at a large red circle, "is where the boat was when Charlie's parents disappeared." It wasn't far from the scattering of islands that dotted the sea around Barbados.

"I asked George to call the harbourmaster and make some enquiries while you were busy blowing things up." (That's Henry – I can never keep anything from him.) "He found out that the *Spinnaker* is still moored in the harbour here. Did you know that 'spinnaker' is the name for a kind of sail used on racing ships to make them faster and more manoeuvrable?" (I didn't.) "Anyway, I got him to pull a few strings and we're allowed to go aboard and check her out. We can be there in half an hour."

I knew that 'pulling a few strings' probably meant that the mighty name of Hunter had been waved about a bit, and marvelled at just how powerful his family were. Since one of Henry's uncles runs the second-largest electronics company in the world, and the other seems to be regularly consulted by presidents and prime ministers about a whole range of things, I suppose it's not surprising. But I found it strange they didn't seem to notice or care what Henry got up to. Maybe they're too busy. Or maybe they just aren't interested. Your guess is as good as mine...

A short time later, George was driving us through the noisy, colourful streets of Bridgetown. People milled around everywhere, yelling cheerfully at each other while cars honked their horns and drivers waved at people they knew. The air coming in through the window was lovely and warm and I wished I'd changed into my shorts.

When we reached the port we thanked George and stepped out onto the dock. It thronged with visitors. I heard so many different languages being spoken I was

completely confused (I'm not great at any of the subjects our teachers as St Grim's think are important, especially languages – which is partly why I love the excuse to get out of lessons by accompanying Henry on his adventures). Unsurprisingly, though, Henry was listening intently, spinning slowly around as he took in everything.

Close up, the *Spinnaker* was even more amazing than in Charlie's photo. I don't know if you've ever been on board a luxury yacht, but let me tell you, they're pretty incredible. Henry told me it was 120-feet long, and it was dotted with spotlights, everything gleaming as if it had just been washed and polished (it probably had). Inside, there were two massive rooms that looked like hotel lobbies, with huge soft chairs and sofas, a separate TV and billiards room, a heated swimming pool (assuming you didn't fancy going in the sea) and even a movie theatre!

Of course, we weren't looking for that kind of stuff, but I couldn't help noticing details — and to be honest there wasn't much else to see, at least nothing that could tell us anything about Charlie's parents' disappearance.

The crew were polite but distant. You could tell they'd been told to be nice to us — but it definitely stopped there. When Henry asked a couple of questions about the trip that the Stevenses had taken six months ago, all he got was a couple of shrugs. Finally, the guy who had introduced himself as Thomas, the first mate, said: "Captain Trueblood comes aboard in one hour. He'll tell you whatever you need to know. Please make yourselves comfortable meanwhile."

We had no trouble doing that, and very pleasant it was, listening to the lapping of the waves and basking on the deck in the warm afternoon sun. A steward brought us Coca-Colas in glasses full of ice and decorated with those little paper umbrella things. *This is the life*, I thought, as I tuned out Henry's chatter about the relative speeds achieved by yachts of this kind and the tonnage of the other craft moored in the harbour.

Just as I was beginning to drift off, Henry leaned across and poked me in the ribs.

"Dolf, I think Captain Trueblood is here."

Reluctantly I prized myself out of the comfortable lounger and followed Henry to the deck rail. From there we got our first look at the owner of the *Spinnaker*.

Captain Trueblood was tall and muscular and had the kind of good looks that my sister (her name is Evangeline, though she understandably prefers Angie) likes to swoon over. His hair was carefully styled to look casual and he wore a lightweight cream suit and a naval-style cap with gold piping round the brim.

Catching sight of Henry and me staring down at him, Captain Trueblood stopped for a moment. For just a second I thought a look of annoyance flashed across his face, but then he waved cheerfully and bounded up the gangplank.

"Nathan Trueblood!" he boomed, stretching forth a large, well-manicured hand.

"You must be Mr Hunter and Mr Pringle – Charles's friends."

While I was still getting used to be addressed as 'Mr', Henry took the proffered hand and shook it vigorously.

"Such a sad business, Timothy and Grace going missing like that," said Captain Trueblood. "And from my boat. I almost feel responsible…"

"We want to help Charlie find out what happened, if we can," Henry explained.

"So you've come all the way from England to find out about 'the ghost ship'?" The way he said this, with raised eyebrows and a knowing wink, made it clear he thought the whole idea was total madness.

"That's one line of enquiry," Henry said rather ambiguously.

Captain Trueblood smiled. "Well, I hope you'll stay and have supper with us," he said. "The chef is cooking up something rather delicious with lobster tonight, I believe." He waved an arm around at the boat. "And do feel free to look around as much as you want. Maybe you'll find a clue to what happened…"

He gave us another knowing look, and it was at that moment that I decided I didn't really like Captain Nathan Trueblood. Henry, however, didn't seem put off. He thanked him politely and accepted the invitation to supper. We watched the captain stride off towards the bridge.

"He obviously thinks we're crazy," I said.

"Does he?" Henry ran a hand through his floppy hair. "I was just thinking he knows a lot more than he's letting on. Being on this boat is still the best way we have of finding out the truth about what happened to Charlie's parents. Trust me, Dolf – we'll have a great time."

Whispers
in the Night

Trust me, Dolf – we'll have a great time! I don't think Henry could have been more wrong.

Supper aboard the *Spinnaker* with Captain Trueblood ranks pretty highly on the list of the worst nights of my life. (OK – I suppose you could say dining with a 1,000-year-old mummy wasn't brilliant either, but that's another story.)

First there was the fact that neither of us was really dressed for a posh dinner aboard a luxury yacht – not even Henry, though he did produce a tie from somewhere – and Captain Trueblood made it clear that it was an occasion by dressing for dinner in an elegant evening suit – bow tie and all.

Then there was the 'something with lobster' that Captain Trueblood had mentioned the chef cooking. It turned out to be a whole lobster, still in its shell and with stalked eyes that I'll *swear* looked at me reproachfully the whole time until I pushed them with my fork so they looked away. It was one of the only times I have dreaded eating a meal.

If you've ever been tempted to eat a fresh lobster, let me tell you now – don't. Apart from the fact that it looks weird, how on earth are you supposed to get into it? I had no idea I was meant to

use the thing
like a pair of
nutcrackers that
was lying on the table
by my plate. Henry knew, of course,
as did the captain, but they both waited just
long enough for me to try and break the shell
using a knife and fork, which resulted in a lot
of strong-smelling fish juice squirting out all
over me!

Although then Henry made a point of
messing about with his lobster claws so much
in solidarity that he made almost as much of
a mess as me. (That's one of the reasons I like
Henry Hunter – he's always on your side, no
matter how much of a prat you're looking at
the time.)

Anyway, if I'd hoped that the conversation
was going to have anything to do with pirates
or treasure or something generally interesting
I was doomed to disappointment. The captain

asked us about school, and about Henry's uncles and their various businesses and, somewhat surprisingly, Henry didn't question Captain Trueblood any more about the night Charlie's parents went missing. I decided to keep quiet, guessing Henry had his reasons. (In any case I was too preoccupied with avoiding any more lobster-juice disasters.)

The dessert course was the only saving grace – it was the kind of ice-cream sundae you would usually get in the best restaurants, and I dug in with relish, although I couldn't help noticing my hands smelled of lobster juice, which almost put me off the creamy caramel ice-cream.

Meanwhile, Captain Trueblood sat back in his chair, clutching a glass of something green and weird-looking. He gazed at us both keenly.

"Well now, boys," he said, "I'm not sure what you expect to find here. Of course, you're welcome to hang out as long as you like, but if I were you, I would forget the whole thing. Of course I feel sorry for poor Charles, and his obsession with the ghost ship he thinks he saw, but I think the best thing is to let him move on. Raking all this up seems like a really bad idea."

He must have been talking to Charlie's Cousin Jack, I thought. I waited for Henry to come back with some strong argument that made it clear he had no intention of forgetting the whole thing, but to my surprise HH muttered, "Perhaps you're right, sir."

I was so surprised I paused with my spoon poised halfway towards the third ice-cream sundae the steward had just brought and stared at Henry. In all the time I had known him I had never heard him agree with a rational explanation for something strange. Usually he was ready to defend even the most fantastical way to make sense of things.

After this no one really seemed to have anything more to say. Henry looked at his watch. "Thanks for the fantastic meal, sir, but it's getting really late. Is there anywhere I can call a cab from here?"

I looked at Henry, confused. Wasn't George coming to pick us up? I was about to remind him of this when Henry nudged me under the table, so I went back to eating my ice-cream. He was planning something, I just didn't know what.

Captain Trueblood looked at his own gold Rolex. "Ah – is that the time? I've kept you up far too long. Why don't you stay the night? There are several empty cabins below. I'm not setting sail until tomorrow afternoon."

Henry put on his most charming smile. "That's very kind of you, Captain." He glanced at me. "OK with you, Dolf?"

I nodded enthusiastically. The idea of sleeping on board a luxury yacht was too exciting to refuse; and to be honest I was feeling a bit stuffed after all that ice-cream.

Soon we found ourselves stretching out in two very large and comfy bunks in one of the grand cabins. I stared up at the ceiling and asked the question that had been on my mind. "Er... you're not really thinking of giving up on this are you, HH?"

"Of course not, Dolf. I just thought it was best to agree with the captain, for now. And I thought that if we stayed on the yacht we may be able to pick up some more clues."

Everything fell into place. Henry had planned for us to stay the night here all along. "So you do think he has something to do with Charlie's parents vanishing like that?" I asked.

"It's possible. Though at the moment I can't think of a motive. I mean, if it was about a ransom he would have asked for it by now. Anyway, Charlie's parents aren't that rich. No," he said decisively. "There has to be something else... something I've not seen."

Suddenly I wasn't quite as keen to spend the night on Captain Trueblood's boat. Thoughts of ghostly pirates, giant squids and kidnappers rattled though my mind. But after Henry fell silent, and lulled by the slight rocking motion of the *Spinnaker*, I soon drifted off to sleep.

The next thing I knew, Henry was shaking me awake.

"What... is it time to get up?" I mumbled.

"No. But something's going on," whispered Henry.

I don't like being woken in the middle of the night, but something about Henry's tone told me that now was not the time to complain. With one leg still asleep, I stumbled out of the bunk.

Henry had his

ear pressed up to the door of the cabin. He beckoned me closer.

"There's someone out there talking to Captain Trueblood. At least I think it's his voice... Anyway, I can hear two people whispering, and I'm fairly sure I heard them mention the Stevenses. This is what we've been waiting for!" HH turned to look at me and his eyes flashed. "Follow me, Dolf – and try to be as quiet as you can."

He opened the door a crack and peered out into the corridor beyond. All seemed quiet at first, but then I heard it too – the rumble of two voices. Henry slipped barefoot through the door and I followed, doing my best not to bump into anything.

We crept along in the gloom. At the end of the corridor a flight of stairs led to the upper deck, and the voices floated down, clearer now.

One was certainly Captain Trueblood. The other was strange: a deep voice with an odd accent that I couldn't place. Strangely, I also thought I could detect a weird burning smell. Or was I imagining it?

"I think I convinced them there is no point in looking any further." That was definitely Captain Trueblood.

"Make sure of it," said the other voice.

There was something about it that made me nervous. It was cold, with no feeling in it at all. Just trying to imagine what the owner of that voice looked like somehow made me afraid. I shivered despite the warmth of the night.

"If there's any doubt, I will take care of them myself," the stranger went on.

"There's no need for that," replied Captain Trueblood, with what I thought was a note

of panic. "No one would believe two fatal accidents so close to each other, and both on board the *Spinnaker*. My reputation would be on the line."

"Then make sure I do not need to," answered the second voice.

A long silence followed, then we heard footsteps crossing the deck away from us.

But only one set of footsteps. *Assuming the footsteps belonged to Captain Trueblood, where had the second person gone?* It was as if they had moved with complete silence – or simply vanished.

Henry nudged me, making me jump. He jerked his head towards our cabin. We tiptoed back and, once inside, with the door closed, he turned to me. I knew the look on Henry's face very well. It meant that he was ready for anything.

"I knew there was something funny going on," he hissed.

"OK. You were right," I said. Then I asked the question that was most pressing to me. "Who do you think the captain was talking to?"

"I don't know," said Henry thoughtfully. "But I'm determined to find out."

DOLF IN THE DUNGEONS

I woke suddenly, a large hand pressed down on my face.

Another hand held my arms in a grip so powerful I couldn't move a muscle. I tried to shout out but a lump of nasty-smelling cloth was stuffed into my mouth. Then everything went black as a bag of some kind was pulled over my head.

All kinds of thoughts went through my head. Words like 'kidnap' and 'ransom', wondering if Henry had been grabbed as well or if it was just me who had annoyed someone sufficiently to make them do this. In any case there was nothing I could do but hope things weren't going to get any worse.

My captor slung me over his shoulder and carried me down several flights of stairs. I felt a warm breeze – we must be outside. I tried to do what Henry had instructed me to do if this ever happened – stay alert for any sounds or clues that might tell me where I was. But the bumping about, together with the rag in my mouth and the sack over my head, made me feel sick, and my brain decided to save me any more discomfort by shutting down for a while.

I woke again to find myself chained to a wall. The bag on my head and the gag had been removed, and I spat and gulped in several draughts of air. I tried to shout, but my voice sounded pitifully thin and all I got in answer was an echo. I had no idea where I was, but I was no longer outside and it was pretty dark. I couldn't even make out a door. Just black walls.

I tried pulling at the chains on my wrists, but soon gave up on that. The links were as thick as my arm and securely fixed to the wall.

I thought back to Henry's advice, and focused hard on my surroundings. I noticed a strong and unmistakable smell of seawater, mixed with something I couldn't identify. It was cold, and I began to shiver. I was dressed for Caribbean sunshine – not so much for freezing dungeons.

I must have fallen asleep a couple of times, each time waking with a start to the realisation that I wasn't dreaming. The cold began to seep into my bones so I did my best to sit up and stretch my arms and legs as far as I was able to keep the circulation moving.

Gradually a greyish light seeped into the place and I guessed that it must be dawn outside. I squinted and saw that I was in a room with walls made of big blocks of stone. The floor was rough earth and the ceiling looked as if it was made of large timbers. The heavy door looked as if it would take a small army to break it down. There were several other lengths of chain hanging from the walls. In fact, the place was so much like my idea of a film-set dungeon that I found myself almost giggling – probably more hysterical than anything.

Then I noticed two bundles of rags leaning against the wall opposite – were there other captives? I shuffled closer, and yelped – they were skeletons, wrapped in a few shreds of clothing. I shuffled back as far away as possible and tried not to hyperventilate. *This is it*, I thought. The realisation hit me like a large wooden mallet.

If these other prisoners had been left to die, their bodies turning into skeletons, surely that was what was meant for me too? For several minutes I struggled like a mad thing to break my chains. When that had no effect I started shouting as loudly as I could.

I've no idea how long I sat there, yelling my head off, but soon my throat was sore and my voice little more than a croak. No one had answered. I slumped down onto the cold floor and rolled myself into a ball. *So this is the end. Forget about cracking* Deathdealers 4. *Forget about any more ice-cream sundaes. There will be no more adventures with HH.*

While I was wallowing in these unhappy thoughts, I heard a noise. I strained my ears. Had I imagined it or were those really footsteps? Then I heard the sound again. Definitely steps, getting nearer.

For a minute I thought about shouting for help again. Then I realised that the footsteps probably belonged to whoever had grabbed me, so I lay still and kept quiet.

The rhythm of the steps changed and I heard whoever it was coming down a flight of wooden stairs. They stopped outside the heavy door and I heard a key being inserted into a lock. Finally the door creaked open (why do old doors like that always have to creak in that spooky way?). A small amount of light outlined a very large figure, but I could see nothing of its face or any other detail.

If you've ever wondered what the phrase 'loomed over' means, I can tell you I experienced it then. The person that entered the room was huge. I mean WWE wrestling-star huge. He was dressed in a dark suit and wore a ski mask that covered most of his face.

He reached out a hand the size of a small football and, grabbing the front of my shirt, lifted me off the ground. He thrust his face close to mine and gave me the benefit of his unpleasant breath.

His eyes gleamed from the holes in the mask and he spoke in a low, gravelly voice with an accent I could not place but which might have been Russian. He kept spacing his words as if he had to think which one to use.

"What... you... know... about... pirates?"

For a split second I thought of making a clever answer about the extent of my general knowledge, but the thought very quickly went away as my captor shook me like a rat and growled: "Tell me... or I... break arms... maybe... legs too... "

"I don't know anything," I said. "So you might as well let me go."

My captor made a funny sound, which took me a while to recognise as laughter.

"You ask... too many... questions," he said. "Boss not happy."

"Well, I'm sorry about that," I said,

wishing my voice sounded a bit less wobbly. "Who is your boss anyway?"

If I'd thought I was going to trick the big guy into giving me information I was disappointed.

"You... must... hope you... not... meet him," said the goon. I thought I detected fear in his voice. If *he* was afraid what could his boss be like?

"Look, we're just here on holiday," I managed. "My friend likes to know about everything. He can't help asking questions." (I thought I might as well stick as close to the truth as possible.)

The goon grunted, then he dropped me suddenly back to the ground with a thud that made my teeth shake.

"Too many... questions," he muttered, still looming. I shut my eyes, wondering what was coming next, but to my surprise the goon moved away towards the door. Risking a peek, I saw that a second figure was standing there, too deep in the shadows for me to have any clear idea of who it might be. The goon joined him and they spoke in whispers.

I strained my ears to hear but all I could get was the word 'captain' and what might possibly have been 'more diggers' – though I wasn't sure about that. Then the second figure left and my least favourite goon came plodding back. He did some more looming, while muttering under his breath and sucking his teeth. Then he said: "No more... questions. I leave you... here... Goodbye."

I had a few moments to think that at least he wasn't going to break my arms or legs before the door thudded shut. Then I realised that I had no water or food (no food!) and that the way my captor had said goodbye sounded pretty final. Then I had much longer to imagine myself starving, shrinking down to nothing, until I ended up like the skeletons chained to the opposite wall.

I must admit that this was one of those times when I almost gave up hope. The likelihood of anyone finding me, even Henry, seemed remote. I slumped down and wondered how long it would take to starve to death – then I remembered that the lack of food was not actually my greatest problem. The average person could only last a day or so without water...

With these happy thoughts buzzing through my brain I must have actually fallen asleep, because the next thing I knew a sound like something

scraping across
the floor above
me woke me with a jolt.

Thinking it could be my captor
returning to do some arm- or leg-breaking
I kept silent at first. Then I thought that
there was at least a chance it wasn't him, and
anyway what had I to lose? I started shouting
again – though the best I could manage was
not much more than a croak.

The scraping noise got louder and, slowly
and creakily, a thin shaft of light appeared
in the ceiling, widening to a square as a trap
door opened above me. I half expected to see
the face of a stranger, maybe the goon's boss,
but I was definitely not ready for the face that
appeared in the opening.

The face of Henry Hunter.

He flashed me his signature grin and
pushed his floppy hair back from his
forehead. "Hang on, Dolf," he said, as calmly

as if he was telling me the time. "We'll soon have you out of there."

The next moment a ladder appeared and slid down until it touched the ground. Henry descended swiftly and hurried over to me.

"You don't look so great," he said, staring at me.

I bit my lip. Now was not the time to worry about such an understatement. I rattled the chains. "They're t-too thick to b-break... "

"Not to worry," Henry replied, producing a lock-pick from his pocket. I'm never sure where he gets these things, or how he always seems to have whatever he needs at any particular moment, but in this case I was just glad. It took him only a minute to pick the lock and free me, then he helped me up the ladder into the light and handed me a thick and not too foul-smelling blanket.

I wrapped it around me. Once I could feel my arms and legs again, and my teeth had stopped chattering, I looked around.

We were in a large room stacked with tottering piles of wooden crates. A skylight let in the sun and I could smell the sea and hear the noisy screeching of seagulls.

"Where are we?" I asked at last.

"In the museum storage area," Henry said.

"Museum... ?"

"The Museum of Pirates and Piracy," Henry said patiently. "In Bridgetown. This is a storage area. Used to be part of the main display from the looks of it, but they must have stopped using it a while ago. Hence your dungeon."

"You mean that was a *fake* dungeon?" I said, putting two and two together. "Well, I can tell you, it's a pretty good one!"

I thought of the two skeletons chained to the wall.

"Were those fake bodies down there as well?"

Henry beamed. "Yep. Just made of resin and rags," he said.

My heart stopped beating quite so hard. "But how did you find me?"

"Actually, it wasn't that difficult," answered Henry. "I was in the ensuite bathroom of the *Spinnaker* when I heard someone enter our cabin. I opened the door just a crack to see what has going on. Whoever it was, he was big, and I knew there was no point in tackling him, so I waited until he was leaving with you and then I followed him all the way here."

"You mean you were there all the time? Well, thanks a lot for not rescuing me sooner!"

"Sorry, Dolf. It was as much as I could do not to get taken myself. He forced the lock of the bathroom – I guess he was looking for me too – and I had to hide in a cupboard with the towels. Seems he wasn't bright enough to look any further. After he'd put you in the dungeon, he hung around for ages. I think he was waiting for someone, because he kept looking at the door. Then I saw him go inside."

"He was too busy menacing me," I said, unable to help shuddering a bit as I remembered the goon doing his looming act and threatening to break my arms.

"What did he want to know?" asked Henry quickly.

"What I knew about pirates," I answered. "He told me if we didn't stop asking questions we'd be in trouble."

"Great!" said Henry. "I was hoping it would rattle their cages a bit."

"Actually, it was me that got the rattling," I said.

"Sorry about that, Dolf. Did anything else happen?"

"Someone else was there. They talked for a bit, but I couldn't hear anything much. Just something about some captain and more diggers… "

Henry frowned. "Diggers? Why would they want diggers?"

"Er... maybe they really are looking for treasure," I said.

Henry stared off into the distance. "You could be right, Dolf," he said at last. "And I wonder who this 'captain' is – our old friend Captain Trueblood, perhaps?"

"The goon said something about his boss. He sounded afraid."

"Well, whoever it was I didn't see him come... or go," said Henry. "I did see your goon heading off, though. I really wanted to go after him, but I could hear you yelling and I thought I'd better get you out first."

Somewhat mollified by Henry's concern, I wondered aloud how they had found us.

"That's why I think Captain Trueblood is involved in all of this," said Henry. "I don't think he wanted us hanging around, trying to find out what really happened to the Stevenses. He suggested we stay on the *Spinnaker* on purpose – so he could arrange for our kidnap to make sure we stay far away from his boat!"

"I could have starved to death down there!" I said. "Please tell me we're going home now?" Even as I said it I knew it wasn't going to happen, but after such a traumatic experience all I could think about was the safety of St Grimbold's.

"We can't leave now," Henry told me. "We're getting closer to the truth. We've got to keep digging. For Charlie's sake."

My stomach grumbled. "Can we at least have a decent breakfast first?"

Henry nodded. "Soon. But can we quickly have a look around the museum, while we're here? We might find some information that could help. Then I promise we'll have a slap-up breakfast."

I knew Henry was right, so I put on a brave face. "OK. But it'd better be interesting."

"It will be. I promise."

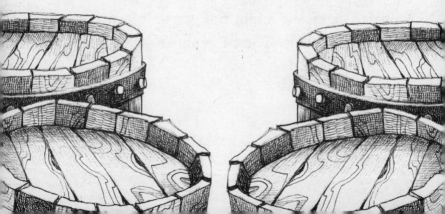

89

In The Museum

For once Henry was right. The Museum of Pirates and Piracy was actually a pretty cool place. For starters we were met at the door by a big bloke dressed as a pirate, who managed to weave just about every cliché you can think of about the subject into his spiel, and kept calling us 'shipmates'. But the best thing about the place was that, when we finally escaped from the piratical guide and went inside, we found that the museum was set up to look as much like the era in which the pirates had lived as possible. We walked along a replica of the Nassau docks accompanied by sounds of waves, creaking timbers and drunken seamen yelling oaths at each other. But the best thing was the main part of the museum, which was set up as a full-size replica of a pirate galleon.

We wandered from deck to deck, looking in at cases of pirate weaponry – plenty of flintlock pistols, long knives, cutlasses and belaying pins (Henry explained that these were wooden pegs used to fasten down the rigging, but also used as weapons), some of which had apparently belonged to real pirates.

Then we came to one of the largest and

most spectacular 3D models I'd seen, showing a pirate captain leading his bunch of fierce-looking seadogs up and over the side of a defenceless trading vessel.

I couldn't help staring at the captain. He was well over six feet tall, built like a brick wall and hung about with weapons. Apart from the big curved cutlass he was holding in one meaty hand, he also had four pistols stuck into the cross-belts that stretched over his large chest. But by far the scariest thing about him was the twists of rope that he had wound into his long black hair. In the diorama they actually glowed as if they were lit. The glow reflected in the figure's black eyes, which seemed to move in his head and follow us. A recording of thunderous explosions and cries and shouts accompanied the scene – it was all a bit too real, if you ask me!

Even though I knew the figure was just a dummy I couldn't repress a shudder. This was definitely not someone you'd want to meet on a dark night. But it was more than that. A strange feeling came over me – as if I somehow knew this character, or had met him already. Perhaps I'd seen him in one of Henry's books?

"Wow! Blackbeard – aka Edward Teach!" Henry said excitedly, coming up alongside me. "One of the greatest pirates who ever lived."

"Pretty nasty-looking bloke if you ask me," I said.

"You're right about that," answered Henry. "He was believed to have killed at least fifty

BLACKBEARD
AKA
EDWARD
TEACH

people, and he sank more ships than any other pirate around at the time. Of course, all he was really interested in was getting rich."

"What are those things in his hair?" I asked.

"Those are tapers," said Henry. "You know, the things they lit to fire their cannons. Blackbeard twisted them into his hair and set them burning before he went into battle. Imagine it," he went on, warming to his subject, "there he was: six feet tall, great big beard, foul temper, with those burning eyes and burning tapers, and all those pistols... No wonder even his crew believed he was in league with the Devil."

"The Devil? What, as in '*the* Devil'... horns and tail and all that?"

"Exactly," said Henry. "Blackbeard escaped capture so often it seemed like more than luck. It's said that when he did finally meet his death he had five bullet wounds and twenty sword cuts on him. In the end, someone slit his throat from behind and then cut off his head."

"Nasty," I said, staring up at the towering figure of Blackbeard. I was glad he was behind glass.

"What's more," said Henry, "after he died his crew reported seeing a sailor on board the ship that no one had ever seen or spoken to. They reckoned it was the Devil himself who'd come to claim old Blackbeard's soul."

"All I can say is I'm glad we don't have to meet him," I said.

"Sometimes I wonder about you, Dolf," said Henry. "I can't think of anything I'd rather do. Meet Blackbeard – that would be something!"

"Something I'd rather not think about, if you don't mind," I said grumpily. But Henry wasn't listening. He had moved away to another glass cabinet.

"Look at this, Dolf. It's Blackbeard's treasure map."

I went and stood by Henry's side. Somehow I still felt as though the figure in the diorama was watching me, making the hairs stand up on the back of my neck, but I dutifully looked at the display. Inside the case was a very old-looking parchment, all stained and ragged around the edges. It showed an island with a very obvious X in the middle, marked in red.

"Come off it!" I said. "You'd think they could manage something better than this. It's got to be a fake."

"Of course," said Henry. "But listen to what it says." He read from the dusty card attached to the window of the case. "A treasure map believed to belong to the dread pirate Edward Teach, also known as Blackbeard, marking the last resting place of his treasure. Many have sought this but none lived to tell the tale. Source: Unknown."

"They must have had fun making that up," I said. "Shouldn't 'dread' be 'dead', anyway?"

"Maybe," replied Henry thoughtfully. "But there's something odd about this."

"What now?" I said.

"Well, everyone knows Blackbeard died in 1718, when the British Navy caught up with him. But look at the card, Dolf. The death date has been scratched out – and recently, by the look of it."

"So – someone was playing a joke," I said.

"This is a museum," said Henry, as if the very idea of someone joking in such a place was impossible to contemplate.

I was about to say something about it not mattering that much but thought better of it. Facts really matter to Henry, at least – for him it's almost an obsession.

We left soon after, Henry still muttering darkly about 'important dates'. He called George the cheerful Rasta to drive us back to our hotel. Henry was unusually quiet on the drive through the busy streets.

"So did we learn anything useful?" I asked at length, still thinking about my extremely delayed breakfast.

"Well, there are at least a dozen stories of pirate treasure hoards buried around the Caribbean," answered Henry, seeming to forget all about his former mood at the chance to spout more facts and demonstrate that he had picked up a lot more information than I had in our time in the museum.

He reeled off a long list of names that

included people with monikers like Black Bart, Ned Lowe, William Kidd and Black Sam Bellamy. (There seemed to be a lot of pirates called 'Black' this and that. Why did you never hear of 'Yellow Tom' or 'Blue Jake', I wondered to myself?)

"All of them have well-known stories," added Henry. "Of course there's no evidence they ever existed." He looked a bit glum at this. "But a lot of people have gone looking for them."

"Including Charlie's dad," I said.

"Yes. Including Charlie's dad," Henry answered seriously.

He was silent for a minute then said, "Just suppose he found something – a clue to some treasure or other. That would give someone a good reason for kidnapping him."

"Kidnapping? Could that really be what happened?"

"It makes sense," Henry answered. "People

have disappeared for a lot less serious reasons. Just like you nearly did," he added, with a grin.

"If it really did happen like that, shouldn't we tell the police or something?" I suggested, thinking that maybe we should tell them what had happened to me.

"Maybe," said Henry. "But we need to find out more before we do that. Right now if we went in with a story about pirate treasure no one would believe us anyway. Not even here."

"Er... So how can we find out more?" I asked.

"We need someone with local knowledge," said Henry. He turned to George, who had, of course, heard all of this, but who, with the kind of discretion shared by employees of Hunter and Co., had said nothing.

"If we wanted to talk to someone who knows everything about this place and what goes on, who would it be?" asked Henry.

"I think I know just the man for you, young sir," said George. "He's a bit rough around the edges, if you know what I mean, but basically harmless."

I wasn't sure I liked the idea of someone who was 'basically' harmless, but Henry was obviously delighted.

"Sounds perfect," he said. "Can you set up a meeting for us – tonight, if possible?"

George promised to do his best and having dropped us at our hotel headed off again into the midday sun.

Back in the hotel room Henry flopped down on his bed and laced his hands behind his head.

"Only one thing bothers me right now, Dolf," he said. "Why was that display in the museum changed? Unless... " He paused with that expression that indicated 'thinking' I knew so well on his face.

"Unless what?" I said.

"The man who snatched you had a key to the museum storeroom, which means he probably works there. And if he has some connection with the place, that's probably why the card got changed."

"What makes you think that?" I asked

"Because it means someone there knows something the rest of the world doesn't. If Edward Teach didn't die when everyone thinks he did, anything's possible. Maybe that map in there isn't a forgery. Maybe it really does show where he buried his treasure!"

I wasn't sure if I followed this line of reasoning exactly, but it certainly made a weird kind of sense. And if Henry was right it could throw a whole new light on the mysterious disappearance of Charlie Stevens' parents.

IRON JAKE

Later, having spent a couple of hours relaxing by the hotel swimming pool, followed by a pretty fantastic supper at one of the restaurants along the quay, George returned to take us to meet our local 'mostly harmless' informant.

"To be honest," he said, as we threaded our way through the evening traffic towards the docks, "I'm not sure what his real name is, but everyone calls him 'Iron Jake'. He's lived around here for most of his life and knows everybody. Nothing happens in Bridgetown without him hearing about it."

"Iron Jake," echoed Henry. "Sounds like a colourful type."

"Oh, he's colourful all right," said George. "But don't let the act fool you. He remembers everything he hears and knows far more than he lets on. If anyone can help you it's Jake."

Personally I was not happy. The name 'Iron Jake' had conjured up all kinds of images in my head – most of them involving us being beaten up and thrown back into that unpleasant dungeon. Henry, however, was obviously delighted and kept leaning forward in his seat to stare out of the windows at the passing throngs of Barbadians, all of whom looked as if they were intent upon enjoying themselves as much and as noisily as possible. We passed chickens in crates, vendors selling hot spicy

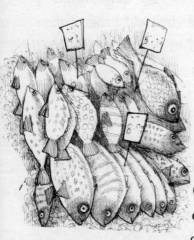

fish and coconut juice – and everywhere tourists trying to find a bargain in the colourful shops that seemed to line every street.

We soon reached the docks, where a forest of masts rose above the water and formed a bristling display against the sky, which was striped every colour from deep red to murky blue. George pulled up in front of a ramshackle-looking cabin, stuffed in between a lobster bar and a shop selling scuba gear. It was a bit quieter here – most people looking for fun along the shoreline gathered around the marina, where dozens of cafes and restaurants spilled their tables out onto the pavement and where the *Spinnaker* was moored.

The cabin looked deserted. No light shone out of its windows and the veranda, which sloped drunkenly to one side, was a pool of darkness. But as we left the car a patch of that darkness resolved itself into a figure that must have been sitting in a battered old chair the whole time.

"Evening, Jake," said George. "This is Mr Hunter and Mr Pringle, the ones I told you about."

"Bit young for treasure-hunters, ain't they?" said the man on the veranda. His voice was gruff and his accent so thick I had a hard time following it.

"We may be young, but we're serious," answered Henry, advancing towards Iron Jake with his hand outstretched.

The man ignored him and as he rose from his chair and emerged slowly into the

flickering light of a streetlamp I saw why.

Iron Jake had only one hand, the other being replaced by a metal fist – the reason, I assumed, why he was called Iron Jake, though it couldn't really be made of iron as that would have weighed a ton. His face was weathered and lined and his hair grey and grizzled. He could have been any age from forty to a hundred. From the way that he moved I deduced that he probably had only one leg as well. As if both these distinguishing features were not enough, he also wore a patch over his right eye. The other eye was very blue and very bright and I could see that it was summing us up pretty quickly.

Seriously, I thought, *could you get any more clichéd than this?*

"I'd ask ye to join me in a tot o' rum," growled Iron Jake, "but I can see you're not of an age for it yet."

"We're good, thank you, Mr Jake," said Henry.

"Just Jake will do," answered our host. "Sit ye down, boys."

George returned discreetly to the car, which I was glad to see was near enough to be able to keep an eye on us without listening in. We sat side by side on an extremely battered lounger, and Iron Jake produced a flask of strong sweet-smelling liquid (rum, I guessed) and took a lengthy swig. Then he lowered himself carefully into his own chair and turned his bright blue eye on us.

"So what can I do for ye, boys?"

Henry outlined the reasons for us being in the Caribbean. When he got to the bit about the Stevenses disappearance, and what Charlie had seen, Jake held up his hand.

"Wait now," he said. "Did you say the name o' these missin' folks was Stevens? Tall fella with red hair, was he, Mr Stevens?"

"Yes," said Henry.

"Aye. I remembers 'em," said Jake thoughtfully. "Came 'ere askin' fer help lookin' for treasure. Weren't too pleased when I told 'im to shove off."

"You must be the person Charlie remembers his dad having an argument with before they left on the *Spinnaker*," said Henry.

"Aye, that'd be me all right," said Jake. "Tis a small world, they say."

He took another nip from his flask and leaned forward, his good eye glinting.

"So this youngster says he saw a black ship with holes in it, flying the Jolly Roger?"

Henry nodded. "He said he could see strange-looking people on the deck as well, but Captain Trueblood... "

Iron Jake snorted. "Cap'n, is it? Trueblood ain't no Cap'n. Just a jumped-up landlubber."

(I did think of putting a list of the odd words used by our informant in here, but I think you'll get the picture.)

"He seemed really concerned about Mr and Mrs Stevens."

"Concerned he may be," grunted Iron Jake. "Mostly that'll be about what he's been searching after these past ten year."

"What would that be?" asked Henry.

"Why the Sword o' Columbus, o' course. Do ye know nothing?"

The idea of Henry knowing nothing struck me as funny, but I smothered my desire to laugh. Henry's ears went a bit red and he leaned forward in his chair.

"I know about the sword, of course, just not that Captain Trueblood has been looking for it."

"He's been following up clues in these waters for a while now," said Jake, taking a sip of rum. "Most folks don't care for him and his ways though. More than one wild goose chase I've heard he's gone on."

"I always thought the Sword of Columbus was somewhere in America," said Henry.

Jake shook his head. "Tis said it were brought here by one o' his lieutenants. There are even those as say it were owned by Cap'n Teach for a while."

"Blackbeard!" exclaimed Henry.

Iron Jake's reaction was instant. He half rose in his chair and jabbed his finger at Henry.

"We don't use that name around here!" he barked. "'Tis unlucky."

Henry was silent for a moment and I took my chance.

"Are we talking about *the* Columbus... the one who discovered America?"

"No one knows for sure if he actually was the first,"

said Henry eagerly, glad as usual to have some knowledge to impart. "Some people think it was a man called Henry Sinclair – who could be one of my ancestors, as a matter of fact, related to the Hunters. But yes, we are talking about Christopher Columbus. When he died his sword, which was said to be a particularly fine blade, vanished. People have been searching for it ever since."

"Aye," agreed Iron Jake grimly. "And that Trueblood fella is one of 'em."

"So what makes you think he had something to do with the Stevenses disappearance?" asked Henry.

"Didn't say as I thought that," muttered Jake. "Just can't be havin' anything to do with him, is all."

"So what do you think happened?" I asked.

Iron Jake swivelled his good eye towards me. For the first time since we had met he seemed reluctant to say anything. Finally he leaned back in his creaking chair and fixed his gaze on the ceiling of the veranda.

"Lost me arm and leg to a shark in them waters out there," he said at last. "Fell overboard durin' a storm. I were adrift fer a day and a night till I were picked up. Fought off that shark with me bare hands. After that I were hallucinating a bit, but I knows what I saw…"

I couldn't help shuddering as I pictured the scene – Jake, minus a leg and an arm, battling a hungry shark in stormy seas. But as usual Henry was more interested in the facts.

"What did you see, sir?"

Iron Jake began to make a strange noise. It was a moment before I realised it was laughter. "Ain't no one called me sir in a long while, young 'un."

Then he was serious again, dropping his voice until we had to strain our ears to hear him.

"Saw a ship, didn't I? All black and flying the Jolly Roger. Saw right though 'er, I did, like she were full o' holes. Came right by me she did, and there was me callin' out to be taken aboard. Glad I wasn't now… "

He fixed us with his brilliant eye. "Let me tell you, boys, I'll never forget what I saw that night. As that ship passed me by – silent as the grave and travelling fast, I saw someone looking over the side at me. Someone big and dark and nasty... Glad I am that I weren't taken aboard that ship. Most likely I wouldn't be here now if'n I had been."

"Who did you see?" asked Henry, when it became clear Iron Jake wasn't going to say any more.

"Not for me to say," he muttered. "Bad luck, I reckon. But it weren't no living man, that's for sure."

Suddenly the warm night air seemed to turn colder. Further down the quay the voices of the revellers faded almost to silence. A wind stirred the palm trees along the shore and the rhythm of the waves along the beach seemed to falter.

"Sir – Jake, I mean," began Henry. "If someone wanted to find out more about this ship, or what might have happened to Mr and

Mrs Stevens, how would they go about it?"

Iron Jake was silent for so long I thought he must have fallen asleep. Then he sighed. "You'd need a craft o' yer own, with a good strong crew and a cap'n as knows these waters well."

"Any idea where I might find such a person?" demanded Henry.

Jake leaned back in his chair and closed his good eye. "If ye are serious, lad, ye can charter me own ship, and her crew. But t'will cost ye. And I won't be guaranteein' your safety."

"That sounds perfect to me," Henry said, as I knew he was going to. He stood up and looked as if he was about to offer his hand again, then thought better of it.

"When and where can you be ready?" he asked.

"Come by the quay in two days' time," answered Iron Jake. "Look for berth number twelve. I'll meet ye there."

Neither of us had much to say on the drive back to the hotel. Henry assured George that the meeting had been, "Very useful, thank you."

As we got out of the car I heard him giving instructions to draw money (quite a lot of it!) from the company funds. If George was surprised he didn't show it. I, on the other hand, was seriously concerned. As soon as we got back to our room I followed Henry into his.

"Are you sure about this, HH?" I demanded. "I mean, we don't know anything about this guy. If you ask me he's a bit weird...

Suppose he just takes the money and then throws us over the side when we're at sea?"

"I think I'm a pretty good judge of character, Dolf," said Henry. "Anyway, who would you rather sail with, Iron Jake or Captain Trueblood?"

Actually I was thinking I'd rather not sail with either of them, but I got the point.

Henry threw himself down on his bed. "Iron Jake may be a bit weird, as you say, but I think he's honest. Besides," he grinned, "how else are we going to get to see this ghost ship?"

Refraining with some difficulty from saying just how much I did *not* want to get to see the ghost ship, I shrugged.

"I'll tell you one thing," said Henry. "I'd rather trust Jake than Captain Trueblood. If Trueblood's been looking for the Sword of Columbus for ten years, that makes him a fanatic. And fanatics are never much fun… "

"I don't see how any of this adds up,"
I said.

"Neither do I – yet," replied Henry.
"Though I'm a beginning to get an idea
or two."

SHIVERING TIMBERS

We spent most of the next day exploring
Bridgetown like normal tourists. It was
Henry's suggestion, but I had a feeling he was
really taking the opportunity to talk to some
of the natives, or maybe to draw out anyone
who might be interested in us. He certainly
made a show of spending some money in the
marketplace. There's no doubt Barbados is a
great place for a holiday – if you aren't being
kidnapped, that is, or looking for people who
probably suffered the same fate. Once or twice
I was convinced we were being followed, but

when I mentioned it to Henry he said I was probably just imagining it.

On the second day we made our way to the quay and looked for berth number twelve. There we found a battered-looking tugboat of the kind that used to haul huge ocean liners into port but that were now (Henry told me) rarely seen in these waters. This one certainly looked as if it should have been classed as extinct some time ago! The name on the prow was *Moby Dick*, though why anyone should want to name their craft after a huge and dangerous white whale was beyond me.

Iron Jake was waiting for us on the dock, smoking a foul-smelling pipe and glaring at the gulls which circled overhead, screaming loudly in the belief that boats + men = food.

"So, ye still want to go a sailin' in search of ghosts then?" he said.

Henry nodded.

"Then ye'd better come aboard." Despite his artificial leg – which, like his false hand, I later learned was actually made of tin not iron – Jake seemed sure-footed enough aboard the little craft. Leading the way to the small, box-like cabin, he introduced us to Joe, a large, silent, unsmiling man with the kind of muscles you generally only see on competitors for the title of the World's Strongest Man.

Joe, we learned, was engineer, first mate and general dogsbody, without whom the *Moby* would not be going anywhere. During the time we were aboard I only heard him speak once, and that was to shout a warning when… well, you'll see when shortly.

Henry was clearly delighted with the sturdy little craft, even though when Joe started the engine a great deal of oily black smoke belched forth. Henry opened his bag and handed Jake a large envelope full of money, which vanished at once into a capacious pocket in the one-eyed man's jacket. Then, we cast off and headed out of the harbour towards the open sea.

Fortunately neither HH nor I were troubled by seasickness. The water was, in any case, incredibly calm, and as Henry and Iron Jake pored over charts in the cabin I looked over the side into the clear blue depths and found it hard to imagine encountering anything dangerous in such a setting.

Which just goes to show how wrong you can be.

We took a course west of the mainland, passing between the islands of St Lucia and

St Vincent and heading out into the waters of the Caribbean proper. Henry had provided the exact co-ordinates for where the *Spinnaker* had encountered whatever it was it had

encountered, and that was where we were heading. It took a few hours of sailing – the *Moby Dick* was not the fastest boat on the ocean – so we whiled away the time watching schools of tiny fish darting this way and that around the hull of the boat, turning and twisting as if they shared a brain.

The water was clear as glass most of the time, and far below we could see the sandy seabed. A couple of times we passed over what were very clearly wrecks, but it became clear to me that such things are not exactly uncommon in these waters and after the first couple of times I stopped embarrassing myself by shouting out "Look – a wreck!" every time.

Around three hours out of Bridgetown we dropped anchor and the regular *thud-thud* of the *Moby*'s engine faltered and died. The silence was intense. Only the calling of the endlessly circling gulls and the slap of water against the hull was to be heard. Somehow, none of us wanted to raise our voices much above a low murmur.

"This is the spot, near as I can make it," said Iron Jake. "See any ghosts yet?"

I thought he was making fun of us, but his face was serious and his bright eye darted about from side to side constantly, as if checking for anything unusual.

From horizon to horizon the sky was clear blue, save for a few fluffy clouds drifting lazily overhead.

So we waited. And waited.

Once we saw a sail on the horizon but when Henry produced a set of powerful Nikon Action binoculars from his pack and trained them on it, it turned out to be a one-man craft with absolutely nothing ghostly about it.

I wasn't really sure what we were waiting for. I had my doubts about ships full of holes and ghostly tentacles reaching out to get us, but then, when you're on a Henry Hunter trip, you never know. Fortunately I'd had the presence of mind to bring a couple of bottles of a vibrantly-coloured drink, mostly made of pineapple, that they were selling at the harbour, so I opened one of those.

At what point the ocean stopped being empty I can't say. Just that one moment we were staring idly at nothing and the next we saw a line of mist spreading across the water. Henry saw it first and trained his binoculars on it. After a minute or two, he lowered them, looking puzzled.

"What do you see, Dolf?" he asked.

"Er… some mist," I answered, wondering if it was a trick question.

"That's what I can see, too," said Henry. "But when I look through the glasses I can't see anything except sea and sky… "

"You mean, like Charlie described?"

Henry nodded.

Here we go, I thought.

Five minutes later, the patch of mist had grown large enough to look menacing, and was grey now rather than white. It billowed about as if it was blown by a strong wind.

Which was odd in itself – because there was no wind.

At the same time I began to catch a glimpse of something inside the cloud. Something big and dark. Henry saw it too, nudging me without saying a word. Apparently Iron Jake did as well, because he left the wheelhouse and joined us at the prow.

"Can't say as I like the looks o' that," he proffered.

Silently I was agreeing, but Henry looked like one of those hunting dogs that show you where the prey is by pointing with their noses – *his* nose was aimed straight at the apparition.

"This could be it," he murmured. "We're about to find out what really happened to Charlie's mum and dad. Come on, Dolf. It's time to find out the truth."

Do we really want to? I was thinking, but I knew this was what we were here for, and it wasn't as if we could go back now.

The mist parted and now we could see what was inside. It was just as Charlie had described: a large old-fashioned sailing ship with black sails, and a black skull and crossbones flag flapping from the main mast. And, again just as Charlie had described, it sported a number of holes along its hull, some large enough to see right through to the waters on the other side.

The calm sea suddenly became very uncalm. One minute we were chugging through dead flat water and the next the *Moby Dick* was rolling from side to side, caught in wild waves that sprang from nowhere.

All of us were caught unawares by the speed of events, even Jake. He staggered sideways and only just stopped himself from being swept overboard by grabbing the rail of the boat with his good hand. At that moment Joe made the only sound I had heard him make since we left Bridgetown.

"Look out!"

Henry and I turned towards the wheelhouse and saw what he had – a huge wall of water, hurtling towards us like an express train.

There was no time to do anything except grab the nearest thing and hang on. Not that it did us much good. The water hit the side of the *Moby* like a battering ram and the little tug virtually stood on its end. I saw Iron Jake, his mouth open in shock, disappear over the side of the boat; then, before I knew what was happening, I was flying through the air, caught in the icy grip of the wave.

Just as I was wishing I had spent more time learning to swim, things got a lot worse. A thin line of brilliant light slashed through the mist and curled itself around me, driving out what little breath I still had in my lungs.

I was hurtling through the icy water and then suddenly I stopped, caught in mid-air. The word 'tentacle' went through my mind and I think I must have screamed.

Then I was slammed against something hard.

I tried to sit up, but quickly wished I hadn't. My head spun and stars flashed in my eyes. I caught a glimpse of Henry a few metres from me and realised we were both on the deck of a ship – but not the *Moby Dick*. This vessel was made of rough dark timbers, cracked and warped, almost as if the ship had been under the sea for a long time.

I was just starting to absorb the horrible realisation of where we were when a pair of feet in tall, black boots appeared centimetres from my face. I tried to raise my head to look up at the owner, but that made my head swim again. The last thing I remembered before darkness claimed me was a cold voice. "What have we here then?" it said. And, as I sank into unconsciousness, I had time to think: *I know that voice.*

I had heard it before...

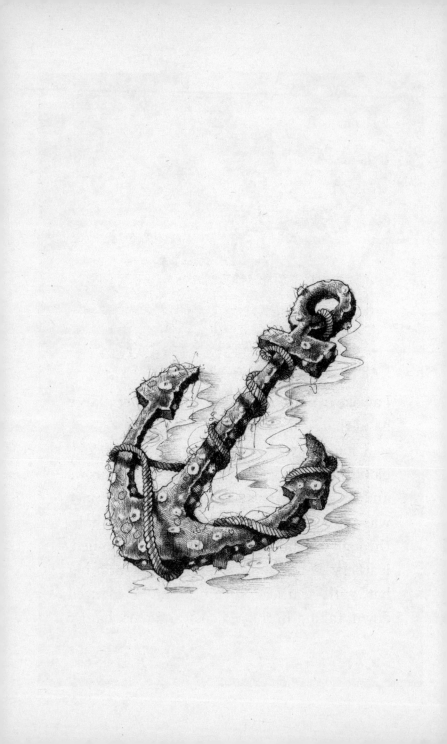

THE CURSED PIRATES

I awoke in mid-air, dangling from a very large hand that held me by the collar.

I found myself looking into a pair of cold, bloodshot eyes, set under huge scowling brows and bristling eyebrows. The rest of the face was mostly covered by thick facial hair, through which I saw glimpses of dark, tanned, leathery skin. Atop the man's head sat a big hat with feathers sticking out. I glanced down, taking in the red coat and dark baggy trousers. My captor looked like he was dressed for a part in a pirate movie. Unfortunately for me, this seemed much more real than a film set. My head was too fuzzy to think properly, but I couldn't help thinking this pirate looked familiar...

His hard eyes continued to inspect me, then the large hand released me and I flopped down onto the deck like a sack of potatoes.

"They'll do," said that cold, dead voice. " Take 'em below, Mr Caraway."

I tried sitting up again. As my head gradually s t o p p e d feeling two sizes too big I looked around and saw about twelve men gathered around us on the deck. All of them were dressed like extras from a pirate movie – stripy jerseys, pistols and cutlasses hanging from their belts. But there the similarity ended. For a start, these pirates looked very real and far from friendly. But the weirdest thing about them was their skin, which was greyish and dull, almost as if they were from an old black and white film.

A particularly evil-looking man with a huge scar crossing his face from brow to chin approached us – I guessed this was Caraway. Alongside him came a little wiry bloke.

I frowned. There was something odd about the way they moved – they seemed to glide, making no sound at all on the deck of the ship.

Caraway had a gold ring in his ear, and the smaller one had tattoos all over his arms, his face covered in pockmarks. Caraway heaved Henry over one shoulder as if he weighed nothing at all, and the other one treated me

in a similar fashion. I dared not scream – I was too frightened, anyhow. They carried us into the depths of the ship and tossed us into a small cage, which couldn't have been more than two metres high and wide.

It didn't smell very good down there, like fish that's been out in the sun too long – sort of damp and cloying at the same time. It was also pretty dark despite the large holes in the sides of the ship. The problem was, there wasn't much light to shine through them. It seemed as if the ship carried its own dark cloud with it. Was that the mist we'd seen?

My head was still hurting and when I tried to sit up everything swam about. Then I heard Henry's voice.

"I'd stay put if I were you, Dolf," he said quietly.

"Where are we, HH, and who was that?" I managed, though my tongue felt several sizes too big for my mouth.

"I'd say we're on board the ghost ship – you recognised him, right?"

"Recognised who?" I asked.

"Come on, Dolf – it's Blackbeard."

"Black—" I stopped myself, realising I had almost shouted the name. I tried again, this time in a whisper: "Blackbeard... you mean the one with the tapers in his hair, the one at the museum?"

"The very same," answered Henry – far too cheerfully, I thought.

"But that means... "

"Exactly. He's dead. Or at least he should be."

"But... " I found I couldn't remember what I had been about to say. The words just wouldn't come out.

Henry said them for me.

"It means he's some kind of ghost. Which is hardly surprising if you think about it – since we're on a ghost ship."

"How did we get here?"

"As far as I can tell we were picked up by some sort of weird tentacle and pulled onto the ship."

"Wh… what do you think it is?" I asked shakily. "Is there a monster hidden away below deck?"

"I don't think so," answered Henry. "I've been thinking about it and I reckon its some kind of ectoplasm attached to the ship."

"Ecto-what?" I said.

"Ectoplasm," Henry repeated. "It's the stuff ghosts are supposed to be made of when they manifest in our world."

"Is that why they seem so… well… solid? I always thought ghosts were supposed to be all wavery, so you could put your hand though them?"

"Not necessarily," replied Henry. "I've

read about some ghosts that are totally solid. And I suppose if they are then the ship can be as well."

"That's because they aren't really ghosts," said a man's voice from the shadows. We both jumped. Peering into the darkness we saw another cage just a couple of metres away. In it were two people. I couldn't see more than that, but Henry spoke up excitedly.

"Mr Stevens?" he said.

"Who's that?" asked the voice, suddenly high-pitched.

"It's me, Henry Hunter. I'm here with Dol – "

"Henry? Is that really you? Gracie, wake up. It's Henry Hunter!"

The second figure stirred in the darkness and a woman's trembling voice spoke. "Henry? How on earth did you get here? Charles... he's not with you, is he?"

"Don't worry, Mrs S," Henry said. "He's safe back home with Cousin Jack."

"Thank goodness. How... how did you get here?" asked Mrs Stevens again.

"The same way as you, I think," replied Henry. "One minute we were on the *Moby Dick*... then we were here."

"The *Moby*?" said Mr Stevens. "Isn't that old Iron Jake's boat?"

"You know him then?" asked Henry.

"Everybody that comes to the Caribbean

looking for treasure knows Jake," answered Mr Stevens. "I tried to get him to help me." A note of eagerness crept into his voice. "Is he with you?"

The question reminded me abruptly of the last time I had seen Jake, mouth wide open, falling backwards off the deck of the *Moby Dick*.

"Not right now, I'm afraid," said Henry, who must have had a similar image in his mind. "We're not sure what happened to him."

"Oh," said Mr Stevens, sounding a lot less happy.

"You haven't told us what you're doing here," said Mrs Stevens.

"Actually, we're looking for you," said Henry. "Charlie didn't believe you were really lost. He asked us to help and, well… here we are."

"You are very brave boys," said Mr Stevens. "But I'm afraid you're in a really dangerous situation. Blackbeard –"

"So it really is him?" I interrupted.

"I'm afraid it is," said Mr Stevens. "And the rest of the pirates seem to be his original crew."

"And they are every bit as nasty as the stories told about them," added Mrs Stevens.

Henry sat forward, not seeming to be the least bit bothered by any of this.

"At least now we know why someone scratched out the death date for Blackbeard in the museum," he said, his eyes gleaming.

"Er… why?" I asked, feeling a bit foolish.

"Because whoever owns the museum knows

that Blackbeard didn't die when the stories tell us," said Henry. "I'll bet you anything Trueblood runs the place... and I'll bet he was the one who sent that goon to grab you, Dolf."

"But why would he be working for Blackbeard at all?" I asked, thinking that no one in their right mind would choose to do that.

"I don't know," Henry replied. "But I'm sure we'll find out soon enough." He looked at Charlie's dad. "You said Blackbeard isn't really a ghost – that none of the pirates are. What are they then?"

"We're not really sure," said Mr Stevens, a grim tone to his voice. "Basically they're dead but not dead – if that makes any sense."

It certainly didn't make any sense to me, but Henry, as usual, was immediately interested.

"Dead but not dead," he repeated. "How's

that possible? Unless they're vampires... or zombies... "

No one said anything for a minute. Then Mr Stevens leaned right up to the bars of his cage and said, very quietly, "They're not vampires and they're certainly not zombies. We think it has something to do with a deal Blackbeard made."

"Deal?" Henry said. "What kind of a deal?"

"The kind that made him the most feared and successful pirate of all time," answered Mr Stevens.

"Ah ha... " said Henry.

My brain was working overtime but I could not work it out. Fortunately, Henry saw my confused face.

"Remember what I told you when we were in the museum?" Henry said. "How Blackbeard was supposed to have struck a bargain with the Devil?"

"You mean that was for real?"

It was Mrs Stevens who answered. She had that wavery note in her voice again. "That's what we think… It's why we're all here. And the others… "

"You mean there are more prisoners?" asked Henry.

I could see Mr Stevens nodding in the dimness.

"At least another four or five," he said. "They're in the forward area of the ship. But they're… not quite the same as us."

"What do you mean, not the same?" asked Henry.

"It's like they're dazed and half asleep," answered Mr Stephens. "They were here when we arrived, and it seems the longer you're on the ship the more likely you are to start forgetting who you are… "

No one said anything for a few minutes after that. But I had more questions. I finally plucked up the courage to ask, "Why? What does he want with us all anyway?"

Neither of the Stevenses said anything and I began to feel little prickles of apprehension doing a dance up and down my spine.

"We're his workforce," said Mr Stephens at last. "It seems that he and his men are only solid when they're on board this ship. As soon as they step off it they turn into wraith-like creatures. Horrible!"

So that must be why we hadn't heard Blackbeard's footsteps when we were aboard the *Spinnaker*. I'd already worked out it had to have been him – the burning smell must have been the tapers in his hair.

I still had more questions. "But what do you mean by workforce?"

"Remember what you thought you overheard in the museum, Dolf?" interrupted Henry. "Something about needing more diggers… "

"Blackbeard is still a pirate, still possessed

with the same greed for gold he always had,"
said Mrs Stevens. "He's looking for treasure –
all the treasure buried by his old friends. He
needs us to dig for it."

WALKING THE PLANK

So there we were – prisoners of the dreaded Blackbeard and his dead-not-dead pirate crew.

We found out just how nasty they could be the day after we had been brought on board the ghost ship.

That morning the pirates hauled Henry and I, and Charlie's mum and dad up on deck to "get some exercise". This consisted of walking round and round the big main mast in the centre of the ship. As well as us there were six more prisoners brought up from the forward hold. All of them, like the Stevenses, had been grabbed a few at a time from Captain Trueblood's vessel by the mysterious glowing tentacle which, as far as we could tell, seemed to be part of the ship itself. They were all adults and judging by their dirty, ripped clothes they had been captive much longer than us. Just as the Stevenses had told us, these prisoners seemed not to understand what had happened to them, and behaved like zombies (not the brain-eating kind, the kind who stare at you in a puzzled kind of way as if they're not sure who or even what you are). It was pretty obvious that they had given up all hope of rescue.

Except for one.

We learned later that his name was Cyrus Firestone and he'd been brought on board only a day or so before us. Unlike the rest of the prisoners in the forward hold he was extremely disinclined to accept his situation. It was that first day aboard, walking round and round the main mast, that we first heard his loud voice.

"I'm an American citizen," he roared. "You have no right to treat me this way! When my government finds out about this they'll send a tactical force to rescue me, and believe me you won't like that!"

Several of the pirates sniggered, and they pushed and shoved the large American wearing a once pristine white suit that was now very wrinkled and stained. He went on protesting and shoved one of the pirates back.

At that point Blackbeard himself appeared. Though Cyrus was almost as tall as him, the pirate captain grabbed him by the collar and lifted him right off the deck, just as he had done with me. Face to face with Blackbeard, the prisoner suddenly stopped yelling and went limp.

"Enough!" barked Blackbeard. He dropped Cyrus to the deck and turned to address us all. His cold eyes swept across his prisoners and he rested a hand on one of his pistols.

"'Tis time ye understood yer purpose here. Ye'll work for me and ye'll do as yer told or face the consequences." He turned away and muttered something to two of the pirates. Then he looked down at us all again. "I'll brook no mutiny on my ship. Those as disobey or cause trouble'll be punished."

The two pirates he had spoken to picked up the dazed American and pushed him towards the side of the ship. At the same time several of the crew began to run out a long piece of wood. It fastened to the deck at one end while the rest hung out over the sea. With a nasty feeling in the pit of my stomach I realised they were going to make Cyrus Firestone walk the plank!

Henry, who was standing beside me, shook his head. "That's strange."

"It's pretty nasty," I said.

"That too," said Henry. "But what's strange is that pirates almost never made anyone walk the plank. It's a bit of a myth. Seems like they've been listening to too many of the stories told about them."

Everyone watched as the man was hoisted

onto the plank and then, accompanied by the jeering calls of the pirates, forced to move along it by pirates prodding him with their sharp cutlasses.

The scene was pretty dismal, but there was nothing HH and I could do. Blackbeard stood glowering down at us from the poop deck (yes, it's really called that – HH explained that it's where the wheel sticks up near the back end of the ship), his huge arms folded across his barrel-like chest. Above us the ragged sails hung unmoving, though the ship continued to plough through the water, moving by some unknown means. The timbers groaned all the time – it sounded as if the ship was in pain.

As the American inched his way along the plank, the plank began to bend – until suddenly, with a cry, Cyrus Firestone vanished, followed by a loud splash, a second later.

The pirates raised a ragged cheer, while

the rest of us looked on dumbly. Then Blackbeard nodded and, to our astonishment, the pockmarked pirate threw a rope over the side. A few minutes later, Cyrus, bedraggled and very subdued, was pulled back on board.

Blackbeard stared down at the rest of us. "Let this be a lesson to ye all," he growled. "I'm bein' merciful... this time. But next time I'll not think twice 'afore I sends any one of ye to the bottom o' the sea."

After that we were all herded back down to our various prisons.

That night Caraway brought us platters of very unappetising food – dry, grey biscuits, which Henry told me were called hardtack, and some stale bread. If we had been offered anything like this under normal circumstances, I for one would have refused it – but by then both Henry and I were so hungry we fell on it like it was a slice of the most

delicious stuffed-crust pizza.

"At least they aren't going to let us starve," Henry said, cramming a handful of the nasty-looking hardtack into his mouth. It was a good point, but it didn't make the food taste any better.

What with the disgusting biscuits sitting inside me like a handful of rocks, the smallness of the cage and the big, black bugs crawling about in the straw, I didn't sleep too well. When I finally did, I dreamed of ice-cream floats and burgers.

BLACKBEARD'S GOLD

The Stevenses told us that the name of Blackbeard's ghost ship was *Destiny's Wyrd*. Henry explained that 'wyrd' wasn't a funny way of spelling weird but that it meant destiny – so the ship's name was really 'destiny's destiny'. That made no sense at all to me, but Henry chuckled – he obviously found it funny.

How the ship kept sailing at all was a mystery. There were rotting timbers everywhere, and large holes probably made by cannonballs. The sails were mostly rags, and the ropes hung like big cobwebs from the masts. Yet *Destiny's Wyrd* sailed on, fast and smooth, surrounded by its own dark cloud. I guessed this meant that no one at sea could see it, but it also meant that we had no way of knowing where we were going.

"I don't understand what's keeping us afloat," Henry said as we walked about on deck for one of our exercise periods. "Everything seems solid enough – including the crew – and the ship keeps moving, even though there's no wind and the sails are a mess. Something must be keeping all of this together."

"What about the deal Blackbeard made – with You Know Who?"

"It could be the reason," said Henry, "but I reckon it's some kind of curse…"

"Curse?"

"At least half the stories about pirate ghosts are connected with some kind of curse," Henry told me. "Usually it has to do with an object they stole that has some sort of strange power."

"So maybe there's some kind of weird object on board?" I suggested.

"Exactly!" Henry exclaimed, eyes bright. "All we have to do is find out what."

"But how?" I muttered.

Henry looked around at the several pirates hanging about, keeping an eye on us. The tall and sombre figure of Blackbeard stood by the wheel, staring out into the mist that surrounded us, as though, for him, it wasn't there.

"We need a diversion," said Henry. "I'll take care of that. The rest is up to you, Dolf... As soon as they aren't looking at us, see if you can get into the Captain's cabin. Look for anything a bit unusual."

My eyes widened – how would I know what was unusual and what wasn't? – but I nodded. I wondered what kind of 'diversion' Henry had in mind and hoped it was a good one.

I soon found out.

We were walking around the main mast in a circle, most of the captives slumping along, heads down, eyes glazed. Even Cyrus Firestone had nothing to say. Since his plank-walking experience he had stopped demanding to contact the American Embassy and generally did as he was told.

As we came to a ladder that led up to the poop deck, Henry suddenly darted up it. The next moment I saw him standing in front of Blackbeard. I heard him say something that sounded like "Excuse me, Captain" and Blackbeard turned with a scowl.

Meanwhile the rest of the prisoners had all stopped where they were to look at HH and so the pirates began to shout at them to keep moving. Three of the crew took off towards Henry and Blackbeard.

In the noise and confusion a couple of the

prisoners tripped over some ropes that were coiled across the deck and fell in a tangle of arms and legs. I glanced up at the bridge again and saw Henry dangling from one of Blackbeard's large hands.

For a moment no one was looking at me.

I was close to the bulkhead with the door that I hoped led to the Captain's cabin. I quietly darted towards it. Luckily, it opened easily and I slipped through.

The room beyond was dark. I made out a big table and a couple of chairs, all bolted to the deck to stop them moving about in rough seas. A cabinet was fastened to one wall and a wooden chest stood beneath the windows.

My heart was pounding so much I was sure everyone on the ship would hear it. My first thought was to look in the chest. I heaved up the heavy lid and gulped.

The chest was full of treasure! Coins, plates and goblets, ropes of pearls, bags of gems and piles of jewellery! I must have looked crazy, my jaw dropped and my eyes bulging, but enough of my brain was still working to remind me of my mission.

Any of these things could be the object I was looking for. Any of them could be cursed. But then I thought: *If there's just one thing keeping the pirates from dying properly then it has to be special. And if it's special, surely it's not crammed into this chest with the rest of this loot...*

I closed the lid and looked round the room. I could still hear noises outside but there was less shouting. I realised that I was going to be missed soon enough and that someone would come looking for me. I didn't like to think what might happen then.

Desperately I stared around the cabin – and caught sight of the cabinet, noticing that one of the doors was not quite closed. I crossed to it and opened it up. Inside, hanging from the back of the cabinet, was a sword – a big straight-bladed weapon that looked nothing like the cutlasses the pirates wore on their belts. The hilt was elaborately engraved and seemed as if it was made of solid gold. Cut deeply into the blade near the hilt were two letters written in an olde-worlde curly script that was really difficult to read. But I was fairly sure they read 'CC'.

CC...

Christopher Columbus! My brain whizzed double-time. Was this really the legendary Sword of Columbus? I looked at it and I was suddenly sure – it gave me a funny feeling, a sort of tingling at the ends of my fingers. It even seemed to have a kind of glow about it – but that could have been my imagination working overtime.

In any case there was no time to linger. Leaving the sword inside, I closed the door to the cabinet and hurried away, slipping out onto the deck. I crouched down behind a barrel and looked out at the scene.

The rest of the prisoners were over by the main mast, guarded by three particularly ugly-looking pirates. At first I could see no sign of Henry, but when I looked up towards the bridge my blood turned to ice.

Blackbeard still had Henry by the collar – only now he was dangling him over the water. I froze. Henry Hunter was going to be thrown overboard!

X MARKS THE SPOT

As I was wondering if there was anything I could do to save Henry if he ended up in the sea – having to battle sharks, rough waves, the bottomless depths of the ocean, the odd octopus – Blackbeard seemed to change his mind. I could see Henry talking to him, but what was more surprising was that the pirate captain seemed to be listening! Abruptly he swung Henry back over the deck and dropped him. He nodded to one of the crew – Caraway – who grabbed Henry and shoved him down the ladder to re-join the rest of the prisoners.

I took the chance to slip out from my hiding place and join them while they were all watching HH.

I caught Henry's eye and he winked, though I thought he looked rather pale.

I didn't have the chance to speak to Henry properly until we were both locked up in our cage for the night. I was bursting to hear what had happened with him and Blackbeard, and what he'd said, but before Henry would tell me anything he insisted that I spill the beans on what I'd found in Blackbeard's cabin.

When I told him about the chest full of treasure he barely raised an eyebrow, simply muttering, "Once a pirate always a pirate." But when I came to the bit about the sword with the golden hilt he stopped me and made me describe it in as much detail as possible. Then he sat back on his heels and regarded me, his eyes sparkling.

"Well done, Dolf! I'm sure that's what's keeping the ship and its crew preserved like this."

"There's more," I explained, for I'd been keeping the best bit until last. "Engraved right near the hilt were the letters CC."

I could almost see HH's brain ticking over.

"The Sword of Columbus?" he yelled, clearly forgetting to whisper for a moment.

"That's what I think," I said excitedly.

"Not so loud, Dolf," Henry shushed me. "We don't want anyone else to know what we know." I raised my eyebrows but decided not to remind him it was he who'd shouted first.

"At least we now know why Captain Trueblood is in league with Blackbeard," he continued. "I reckon he thinks he'll get the sword somehow if he brings enough people for Blackbeard to use to dig up all that treasure."

"Do you think Trueblood knows it's the sword that's keeping him alive – Blackbeard, I mean?"

"No idea," said Henry, "Trueblood probably just wants the sword because he thinks it will make him rich. I suspect we'll find out pretty soon, one way or the other," he remarked mysteriously.

I wasn't sure I liked the sound of that, but I knew it was useless trying to get Henry to say more until he was certain. Instead, I asked him what had happened when he'd spoken to the terrible captain.

Henry grinned. "I went up to him and addressed him by his proper name – Captain Teach. I think that got his attention, or maybe he was just surprised that any of us would try to talk to him. He didn't say anything right away, just stared down at me like I was something he'd scraped off his shoe. So I went ahead and asked him what it was like to stay alive for over three hundred years. I wanted to keep him distracted while you got into the cabin, so I asked if he missed his old mates or if he got bored sailing about on *Destiny's Wyrd* for years on end.

"The next thing I knew I was dangling over the water while he glared at me and told me I was a foolish puppy and asked if I'd like to feed the fish… "

"What did you say that made him change his mind?"

"I apologised if I had offended him but said I had heard so much about him and that I was a real fan. Then I mentioned a couple of famous events from his life and that seemed to calm him down. I think he was actually pleased. Always appeal to the bad guy's ego if you're in a tight place, Dolf. They usually can't resist a bit of praise. Anyway, that was when he stopped dangling me overboard."

"Lucky you knew so much about him," I said.

Henry grinned. "Are you actually telling me you think knowing stuff is useful, Dolf?"

I went a bit red. Sometimes I have to admit I'm a bit hard on HH about all his knowledge. This incident proved how valuable it could be. I resolved there and then to listen more carefully to what Henry had to say in future – assuming there was any future, of course.

The next day *Destiny's Wyrd* dropped anchor. We had no idea where we were, or even in which direction we'd been sailing. The cloud of mist put paid to any chance of discovering that. All I could tell from where I sat in the cage was that we had stopped moving, and I thought I could hear the cries of gulls. I knew that usually meant we were near land.

Then Caraway appeared and unlocked

our cage, and the one containing Mr and Mrs Stevens too.

"Up ye go!" he growled, shoving us towards the deck.

I was surprised to see the mist had thinned – we were anchored close to the shore of what looked to be a small island. It was edged with a strip of golden sand, beyond which lay a line of palm trees and then thick, tangled undergrowth.

To be up on deck with solid ground in sight made me feel a lot better – though I wondered what was coming. Digging for treasure for Blackbeard, if the Stevenses were right.

When all the prisoners stood together in the shadow of the poop deck, Blackbeard appeared and glowered down at us.

"Listen well," he growled. "You'll all be

goin' ashore, and there'll be diggin' to do. Diggin' for treasure. My treasure! But don't ye try anything foolish like runnin' off. This island is only a few leagues long and even fewer wide and it's a long way off the trade routes – so no other ships are likely to come this way in a long while. If ye want to see home again, ye'll work as hard as ye can to get my treasure."

No one said anything. The rest of the prisoners looked as dazed as ever. Even the Stevenses were starting to look that way. I wondered how long it would be before Henry and I started feeling zombie-like too, and hoped we might somehow be immune. Otherwise we had no chance of ever getting away from Blackbeard.

Caraway and Pockmark issued us all with

shovels and sacks then pushed and shoved us towards a little rowing boat (apparently called a jolly boat – not that there was anything funny about it).

Just as we were about to get in, Blackbeard beckoned Henry to him. "Since ye know so much about me and my life, I'll give ye the honour of being the one that carries this," he said in his cold voice that made all the hairs on the back of my neck stand up.

He handed Henry a rolled-up piece of parchment. "Follow the instructions and ye'll find the treasure. And see ye get up to no tricks – or else."

It only took a few minutes of rather inexpert rowing to get us to the shore. We stumbled onto the land like a bunch of drunken people. It felt weird to be on a surface that wasn't constantly moving. But we were alone – for the first time in weeks there were no pirates watching our every move.

Henry unrolled the parchment.

If you've ever seen a drawing of a pirate treasure map you'll have an idea of what we were looking at. Lots of wavy lines and little pictures of palm trees and landmarks, and sometimes a few directions like *Walk ten paces, turn left and walk five paces, then dig.* It even had a big red X in the middle.

"Where do we go, Henry?" Mr Stevens asked, excitement in his voice. He suddenly looked a lot less dazed than he had done on board the ship. I understood why. After all, he had been hunting for pirate treasure for much of his life and now, here he was, actually about to dig some up. The fact that he was Blackbeard's prisoner didn't seem to matter right now.

HH studied the map carefully, glancing up at the skyline and towards the edge of the trees, where dark shadows pooled. I hoped he was thinking about how we might possibly escape. It had to be possible, didn't it?

"That way, I think," he said, pointing towards an almost invisible track that led off into the jungle.

We began heading in the direction Henry had indicated when something happened that stopped us in our tracks. Two of the cursed pirates joined us.

TREASURE!

The possibility of escape suddenly seemed a lot less likely. Behind us were Caraway and Pockmark – although they looked a lot different now.

If I say they were mere shadows of themselves you'll get the idea. They looked like shreds of drifting smoke, and I could see right through them. They seemed to have no legs or feet – just ragged strands of darkness that trailed slightly above the ground. Even their faces looked thin and insubstantial – except for their eyes, which glowed like hot coals.

They looked a lot more like my idea of ghosts than they did when they were aboard the ship. Not very nice at all, I can tell you. The pirates seemed unable to speak in this form – they could only make unpleasant hissing noises like a threatening snake. But with those glowing eyes trained on us, they made it pretty clear by pointing at the map, then straight ahead, then at the map again, that they expected us to get on with finding the treasure.

So with Henry leading the way we entered the jungle. The light was greenish and the air warm and sticky; the undergrowth on both sides of the narrow trail was virtually impenetrable. Together with the bugs that were soon biting everyone and the ominous rustling sounds, the place was far from wonderful. I started to wish I was back on the ghost ship.

The cursed pirates followed us, as if they were afraid we would steal their treasure –

though I'm not sure what they thought we would do with it.

Most of the time the path, turning and twisting, climbed steadily. We had waded through thick undergrowth for about two hours, I guessed, before Henry stopped and pointed to the big red X on the map.

"We're almost there," he said, striding on and emerging into an open space.

We carried on, awash with sweat by now, tired and bitten to death. From there the path climbed a few hundred metres further to an opening in the rockface.

Henry consulted the map again. "It looks like the treasure is hidden in that cave," he said.

The ghostly pirates were clearly excited, waving us on and hissing a lot as we shuffled towards the entrance of the cave, which was really little more than a crevice between two

big rocks. Henry scavenged some bits of dead tree root and lengths of creeper vine, tying them together to make a rough torch. Then he produced a box of matches that – don't ask me how – he had not only managed to hang onto since our capture but which, even more amazingly, still worked!

The torch smoked a lot and didn't smell that great but it gave us enough light to see by as we entered the cave.

We all squeezed in. Henry raised the torch and my eyes widened. By its jumping, flickering light I saw that we were not alone.

Well, in a manner of speaking, anyway – because the two people already occupying the cave were not only dead but, unlike Blackbeard's crew, looked as if they'd been that way for some time. Their skeletons lay propped up against the back wall of the cave. I realised they were both clutching cutlasses, the blades of which stuck out of both bodies around the area of the rib cage.

I shuddered – if I had been frightened by the fake skeletons at the museum, these terrified me. Henry however marched over and took a really close look at the two bodies.

"I'll bet these are the ones who buried the treasure," he said. "Perhaps they fell out afterwards and killed each other."

I imagined a grizzly image of the two men struggling desperately, stabbing each other at the same moment. But Henry had already moved on to examining the floor of the cave.

"This bit has definitely been disturbed," he said. "I think we should dig here."

If it hadn't been for the fact that we were prisoners of the infamous pirate Blackbeard and that there were two scary dead men hounding us, this could have been pretty cool. As it was, we were all hot, tired and nervous – not to mention itchy from all the insect bites.

We dug in silence. The dazed prisoners

barely spoke any more anyway. Several blisters later, our spades hit something hard.

"Aha!" Henry remarked. I was just glad we might soon get to stop – I was exhausted.

It took a few minutes to uncover the lid of a wooden chest and dig around it enough to drag it out onto the floor of the cave.

Of course it was locked – and of course Henry wanted to smash the lock and take a look inside.

I had my doubts that was a good idea, but Mr Stevens was as excited as he could

possibly be, under the circumstances. "Open it, Henry," he said.

Henry hesitated for a moment. Then he said, "Well, they did give us these sacks, so they must intend us to fill them with whatever's inside! He grinned. "I for one am not going to do all this digging and not know what's in there. It might be full of rocks!"

He had a point. As no one had anything more to say, Henry gave the chest a thump with his spade. The old wood groaned and he hit it again. This time the bit around the lock split open with a crack. Henry lifted the lid and we craned to look inside. My heart pounded with excitement. Pirate treasure! Even the dazed prisoners peered in and Mr Stevens looked as if he was going to faint from excitement.

Needless to say the chest was not full of rocks. It was, in fact, bulging with coins, jewels and some old plates and cups – all made of the same shiny stuff. No one said anything. We all just stared. I think we might have stood there for a long time, but eventually Henry slammed down the lid of the chest with a bang that made everyone jump.

"OK," he said. "Let's get this outside. Our floaty friends will be wondering what we're up to."

It was only then that I realised the two cursed pirates had not come into the cave with us. Had something about the place kept them out? Maybe they had once known the skeletal sailors? Maybe it reminded them that they were actually dead? In any case, they were waiting for us as we hauled the heavy chest outside. Their red eyes seemed to gleam all the brighter and the hissing noises got louder, which seemed as near as they could get to cheering.

Gold is heavy stuff, and I was glad of the sacks we had been given before we left the *Destiny's Wyrd* so that we could spread the load between us. We emptied the chest and filled the sacks as fast as we could.

While everyone was busy, Henry pulled me to one side.

"Listen, Dolf," he said. "On the way back to the ship we're going to make a break for it."

"But they'll see us, won't they?" I exclaimed. "And if they do they'll leave us here alone without food and water!"

"We're not going to be left behind," said Henry. "And I don't think we're alone, anyway."

"What!" I said, probably too loudly, because Henry shushed me.

"Didn't you notice all that rustling in the underbrush?" Henry asked. I had, of course, but I'd been thinking of large scary animals.

"You mean someone's following us?"

Henry nodded. "Almost since we left the beach. I thought it was monkeys or something at first, but there was a glint of something metallic – and to my best knowledge birds or animals don't carry anything made of metal."

"So what's the plan?" I asked, resignedly.

"Once we get back into the jungle, fall behind a bit. As soon as the others are out of sight we'll get off the path."

I thought of the thick undergrowth, where anything could be lurking. But I knew it was no use arguing with Henry; he had that determined look he gets when we are up to our eyes in trouble and he's thought of a way out.

Once the treasure had been transferred into bulging sacks the cursed pirates made it clear they expected us to get a move on and head back to the ship. There was a bit of grumbling among the adults, which showed they were actually beginning to wake up – maybe because they were no longer on the ship. I heard Cyrus Firestone say something about 'slave labour' but the two ghostly shades flew around us in circles, glaring and hissing and pointing until finally everyone swung a sack over his or her shoulder and began to stumble back down the slope towards the beach and the waiting ghost ship.

Fortunately for Henry's plan, Caraway and his chum Pockmark were so eager to show off the haul (as if they had done all the work instead of hanging about outside the cave!) that they went ahead. I suppose they thought there wasn't anywhere much for us to go so they weren't worried.

They didn't know Henry Hunter. As soon as we were deeply into the jungle Henry dropped back, allowing the rest of our little party to get ahead. At a bend in the path he slipped sideways into the heavy foliage, beckoning me to follow. In fact, the undergrowth wasn't as impenetrable as it looked, and within minutes we were several feet from the path and well hidden. Henry stopped to wait for me and we both dropped our sacks, which were a bit lighter than everyone else's thanks to the fact that we were smaller and younger.

"So what happens now?" I hissed, as quietly as I could.

"We wait," said Henry cheerfully, slapping another thirsty bug out of existence. "For whoever it is that's been following us to put in an appearance."

We didn't have to wait long. After several minutes of listening to the 'zing' of insects and the far-off chatter of birds in the canopy of the jungle, there was a rustling sound off to one side and, while I was still wondering what we would do if it turned out to be something big and nasty with razor-sharp claws and pointy teeth, the bushes parted and a face looked through at us.

I let out an involuntary yell and once again Henry had to shush me. To be fair, even HH looked pretty amazed to see who it was that had been following us. Probably the last person in the world we could have expected – considering that the last time we had seen him he had been falling backwards off the deck of the *Moby Dick* into the depths of the ocean.

An Unexpected Meeting

"Jake!" Henry and I exclaimed almost in unison.

"Aye," answered Iron Jake, actually grinning at us.

"But... I thought... " I stammered. "I mean... I saw you falling into the sea. How could you have escaped?"

"Takes more than a bit o' water to drown me," Jake answered. "Though I has to admit I did get a bit o' help, or I might be feedin' the fishes right now."

"Help?" put in Henry. "What kind of help?"

"Well, that's a long tale," said Jake. "But I'll keep it short, seein' as we don't have much time." He cleared his throat and I thought he looked a bit uncomfortable, as if admitting he'd needed help of any kind wasn't something he did easily.

"When I fell off the deck I thought me time'd come. I knew the ocean was pretty deep there, and what with me hand and me leg weighing a bit I didn't reckon as I'd be floatin'. Nor did I. I sank like you'd expect and began to think I'd be meetin' Davy Jones a lot sooner than I'd planned."

He paused for a moment and looked thoughtful. "I seen a good few strange things in my time but nothin' like what happened then. Just when I started seeing bright lights and my lungs felt like they was going to bust, I felt meself grabbed and then I was heading back upwards. I broke the surface and took a few lungfuls o' good clear air afore I looked to see what had rescued me. And blow me down if it weren't a mermaid."

"A what?" I said, probably looking about as disbelieving as I felt. Jake didn't look like he'd been drinking, but I remembered his liking for rum.

"Aye," said Iron Jake. "I weren't sure if I hadn't just drowned and were seeing something that weren't there. But no, sure as I'm talking to you now, it was a real-life mermaid. All fins and scales and long green hair."

"But I thought mermaids were imaginary!"

"Come on, Dolf," interrupted Henry. "How many times have I got to tell you? You can't be sure whether a thing's real or not until you've seen it. Didn't you once refuse to believe in vampires?"

"But I *haven't* seen a mermaid," I said. "Not yet anyway."

"No need to argue, boys," said Jake. "All ye needs to know is that 'twas a mermaid saved me. Brought me up near where I fell in. I could see everything that happened – the ghostly ship and you two lads being pulled aboard."

"But how did you get here?" asked Henry.

"That were the mermaid again," said Jake. "Swam after that ghosty ship for four days carryin' me on 'er back and never once complained."

Jake suddenly frowned. "I don't mind sayin' as how I got words to say to that nasty lump o' fish-bait as scuppered my ship – and like as not drowned Joe. I seen him, struttin' about on the deck like he were something fancy…"

"You know who he is then?" said Henry.

"Oh aye, I seen pictures of him enough

times to know old Cap'n Teach when I sets eyes on 'im. Ought to have been sent to Davy Jones long since."

The old sailor had clearly said all he was going to about his adventures, and right then there wasn't time to consider the possible existence of mermaids. Instead Jake looked at us expectantly. "So what's the plan, boys?"

"Not exactly a plan," Henry said. "But I've got a few ideas."

While I was wondering whether this was the only time I had ever heard Henry Hunter admit that he didn't have a plan, he launched into the story of our adventures since being taken aboard the *Destiny's Wyrd*. When he got to the part about my daring discovery of the Sword of Columbus (well, it was a *bit* daring!) Jake stared at us with disbelief.

"You mean that sword is on board the ghosty ship?" he said.

Henry nodded. "The question is, could it

be the reason why Blackbeard is still sailing the Caribbean?"

"Like as not," nodded Jake. "Like I told 'e, I've heard tales about that sword. Seems the hilt were made of gold from the Amazon. Columbus took it from the natives and one of them put a curse on it. Seems like the curse must have been carried over when the gold was made into the hilt of his sword."

"So what can we do, then?" I asked, when both the others seemed sunk in thoughts of the sword.

Finally Henry looked up. "I have an idea," he said.

There it was, HH to the rescue!

"We've got to get the sword and send it to the bottom of the sea. Send it to Davy Jones's Locker."

I nodded. It seemed so simple when Henry

said it, but I was still a bit confused.

"Er... how exactly will that help us?"

"Aye?" echoed Jake.

"Well, if my theory is right, the pirates and the ship will disappear once the sword has gone."

"But what will happen to us?" I had a horrible image of us sinking to our deaths as the ghost ship holding us afloat dissolved into nothing.

Henry grimaced. "That I'm not so sure about. But as far as I can see, it's the only way we'll escape Blackbeard."

"How are we going to do it?" I asked, groaning inwardly. "The sword's hidden away in his cabin."

"First we have to get Jake on board the *Destiny's Wyrd*. Then we'll have to see if we can arrange another diversion."

"Last time you did that, Blackbeard let you off with a warning. If you try something like it again you might not be so lucky!"

Henry shrugged. "Has anyone else got a plan?" he asked.

Neither Jake nor I had anything to say.

"Right then," said Henry. "Let's go. We'll be missed if we don't catch up with the rest of the party."

We hurried back towards the beach, only pausing long enough to collect the heavy sacks from where we had left them. Jake showed a lot of interest in the story of the treasure chest, which we related as we followed the twisting path back through the jungle.

"Reckon as I'm owed a bit o' that gold," he grunted, as we made the best speed we could. "Payment for the sinking of the old *Moby Dick* and the loss o' her first mate."

I felt sad for a moment as I remembered Joe, but there wasn't time to dwell on it. Amazingly, it seemed no one had noticed our temporary disappearance. We managed to catch up with the tail of the party, and Jake joined up with us. For the first time I was really glad that the adult prisoners were so out of it, so that none of them seemed aware of the presence of an extra man. Jake tucked his metal hand inside his shirt and at the last minute Henry gave him his sack of treasure too, while he himself sauntered along holding the map as if he had never had anything else to carry.

The pirates were clearly far too interested in the treasure to notice, or to count the number of workers they returned with. After all, no one was missing, and who would *choose* to go aboard Blackbeard's ship if they didn't have to? We rowed across while the two ghostly pirates hovered over us, encouraging us with gestures to make the best time we could.

MEN OVERBOARD!

Back on the deck of *Destiny's Wyrd* we were instructed to pile the sacks of treasure in a heap. Blackbeard oversaw this himself, with a gloating look in his dark eyes, while all the other pirates watched on, engrossed. When we'd finished, Blackbeard addressed us – hands on hips, with his big beard bristling and enough pistols stuck into his belt to kill a small army.

"Ye did well today. Soon, there'll be more

o' ye to help with the diggin'. If ye keeps on bein' this obedient I might even spare your worthless lives – after I've collected all the treasure that lies hid about this ocean."

Henry nudged me. "More prisoners coming," he whispered. "That probably means the *Spinnaker* will be bringing them. That could be our chance!"

Suddenly, things didn't seem quite so desperate. Was Henry right? I really, truly hoped so. At least we had Iron Jake on our side. He had vanished somewhere after we came aboard. Wherever he was hiding I hoped Blackbeard didn't find him.

Once we were locked back in our cell Henry outlined his plan.

"We've got just one crack at this, Dolf. We have to get the Sword of Columbus away from Blackbeard and get rid of it, preferably over the side into the sea. Then we can get back on board the *Spinnaker* and take care of Captain Trueblood."

Henry called across to Mr and Mrs Stevens to tell them the plan.

They nodded vaguely.

"Be careful, boys," Mr S told us with vacant eyes. "That Blackbeard is... a nasty piece of work."

About as nasty as they come, I thought. But Henry wasn't fazed.

"We do this kind of thing all the time, don't we, Dolf?"

I nodded, wondering what 'kind of thing' he was thinking of. The kind that generally involved us getting into danger, I guessed.

As it happens, I was right.

We heard the bumping of the treasure-laden sacks being dragged away below and into the hold. Soon after, the *Destiny's Wyrd* set sail again, and soon after *that* we heard a shuffling in the dark and Iron Jake's face appeared out of the darkness, grinning at us.

"OK, boys?" he asked. "Ready fer action?"

Actually I was feeling very far from ready.

Tangling with Blackbeard wasn't my first choice of action, but Henry clearly couldn't wait. "Once Trueblood arrives, Dolf," he said, "you and Jake need to cause enough of a distraction to cover me."

"What sort of distraction?" I asked, hoping it wouldn't involve Blackbeard dangling me over the ocean.

"Anything will do, as long as you make plenty of noise and keep the crew busy."

"I think we can manage that," said Jake with a conspiratorial wink from his good eye.

"What about the rest of the prisoners?" I asked.

"We can't count on much help from them," Henry answered. "The best thing will be to wait until we're all on deck for our exercise and then make our move. Hopefully there'll be enough confusion for me to get into

Blackbeard's cabin and get the sword."

As plans went I thought it wasn't one of Henry's best – but under the circumstances there's wasn't much else we could do.

Neither of us got much sleep that night, and for once it had nothing to do with our uncomfortable quarters or the nasty insects crawling over us. All I could think about was the fact that we were taking on the most fearsome pirate who had ever lived. The fact that he and his crew happened to be dead made it worse, as did the fact that I knew we couldn't count on any help from the rest of the prisoners. I wasn't even sure Charlie's parents would be any use now. That left just Iron Jake. I hoped he was good in a scuffle.

The only thing I could do to make myself feel any better was to remind myself that Henry and I had been in worse scrapes before and survived. (We had, I promise you. Try being shut up in a tomb with a really annoyed Egyptian mummy and you'll get the idea.)

The next day, Henry and I waited patiently, albeit nervously. Would the *Spinnaker* appear? We dropped anchor somewhere in the middle of the open sea, and we both peered through one of many holes in the side of *Destiny's Wyrd*.

Sure enough, a shadow in the mist announced the arrival of the *Spinnaker*. Huge waves began to batter about us, and we could no longer see what was happening through the spray and the mist. I guessed it was the same thing we had experienced – those on board the *Spinnaker* were being thrown off and taken onto *Destiny's Wyrd* by that slithering, evil tentacle. Finally the rocking of the ship calmed, and we heard the booming voice of Captain Trueblood, followed by the cold, gravelly tones of Blackbeard. Soon after, Pockmark came to unlock our cage and usher us above deck for our daily exercise, scowling all the while.

The dull circle of the sun, which was all we could see of it through the mist, was already low on the horizon. The *Spinnaker* rode at anchor alongside us and Blackbeard and Captain Trueblood stood by the wheel of the yacht, deep in conversation. On the deck of *Destiny's Wyrd* were two new prisoners, an adult couple who looked bewildered and terrified, pushed and shoved in among us by grinning pirates.

Henry and I mooched along with all the rest, circling the deck around the main mast, keeping our heads down. I couldn't see Jake anywhere, but hoped he was hiding close by. As we passed the poop deck for the twentieth time, Henry turned to me. "OK, Dolf, next time we pass this point it's time to make your move."

I'd had a whole day to think of what I was going to do, so I was as ready as I was ever going to be. I began to stagger about and then fell on the deck, clutching my stomach and howling as loudly as I could. It wasn't my best performance ever, but it got the attention of the pirates. Even Blackbeard turned to look and I saw Captain Trueblood staring over towards me with an annoyed glare.

Then everything went crazy.

One of the pirates came across and poked me with his foot. I grabbed hold of it and heaved with all my strength. The surprised man fell back onto the deck with a grunt (I have to admit I was rather surprised, too). I jumped up, swarmed the ladder to the poop deck, then launched myself at Caraway.

"You scar-faced, evil pirate! How dare you kidnap us and use us for your own treasure-stealing!" I shouted.

Taken by surprise, Caraway fell beneath me with a yell. I was glad he softened the landing. I heard Blackbeard chuckling with laughter and looked over my shoulder. Somehow he had crossed back from the deck of the *Spinnaker* and stood, hands on hips, rocking backwards with merriment. Despite the laughter he looked even nastier than when he wore his usual grim expression.

Of course it only took a few moments for the pirates to grab me. Two of them jerked me to my feet and held me like a sack of potatoes. I stopped howling as soon as I saw that Henry had vanished – hopefully into the captain's cabin. I wondered what had happened to Jake. Had he been captured, or had he decided not to help at all?

"Enough!" Blackbeard snarled. "Any more o' this noise and I'll see ye all feed the fishes."

I'd heard it before, and I was pretty sure the threat to throw us overboard was an empty one since he needed us to dig for treasure, but it seemed no one wanted to risk it. Silence returned.

Caraway was holding a handkerchief to his nose, which was bleeding from my attack. I couldn't help but smile – I never thought I could win a fight with someone as big and scary as that. Everyone else just stood there; the prisoners were as bewildered as ever, and the pirates seemed uncertain what to do next, though I could see that some were fingering their cutlasses – probably in the hope that their captain would give them permission to kill someone.

Out of the corner of my eye I saw Henry sneak out of the captain's cabin, carrying the Sword of Columbus. He made his way towards the side of the ship, keeping to the shadows.

Unfortunately, someone else saw him too.

Captain Trueblood.

The sight of Henry carrying the object

he'd been looking for all these years must have come as a horrible shock. Perhaps he had not known the sword was on board *Destiny's Wyrd* until that moment, or maybe Blackbeard had promised to show him where it was in return for his help.

As it was, Trueblood gave a yell that was probably heard all the way back in Barbados. He launched himself across from the *Spinnaker* and hurtled after Henry. Blackbeard, seeing what HH was holding, also bellowed with fury, drawing one of his pistols. He took aim at Henry and cocked the hammer.

I had to do something. Henry would surely be killed. With the pirates holding me distracted, I managed to pull free and throw myself at Blackbeard. (I know you're thinking 'this is not like Dolf', but sometimes you just have to do what needs doing. At least that's what Henry Hunter always does, so that's what I did too.)

I'm not sure what would have happened next. I'm not exactly a heavyweight and Blackbeard was huge, but fortunately for me, at that moment Jake chose to make his move. He leapt out from where he'd been hiding and, moving with considerable speed for a one-legged man, he flung himself at the pirate captain, knocking his arm to one side.

Attacked from two directions at once, Blackbeard was taken by surprise. His pistol went off with a loud explosion and the bullet ploughed a furrow in the deck just a few centimetres from Henry. Blackbeard swung a fist the size of a leg of lamb at Jake, who grunted and fell back onto the deck, out cold.

Henry, meanwhile, skidded to a stop and everyone on the ship froze. It was one of those moments that seem to go on for a long time but is actually over in less than a nanosecond.

Everyone's eyes were on Henry Hunter.

The pirates, who were determined to

get hold of him...

Blackbeard, who looked about as mad as I've ever seen anyone...

Captain Trueblood, who had *his* eyes on the Sword of Columbus, as though it was the most precious thing in the world...

And me, because I was suddenly afraid that we were in the worst mess ever...

Then everything started happening at once.

Blackbeard rushed at Henry waving a very large cutlass. Captain Trueblood stood there as if his feet were glued to the deck, his eyes almost popping out of his head.

Then Henry did something very silly. He raised the Sword of Columbus and swung it at the pirate captain.

Blackbeard turned the blow aside as easily as if a wasp had tried to sting him. Henry fell backwards and the sword flew from his hand, curving into the air, where it seemed to hang still for a moment.

Henry somehow recovered his footing, jumped up onto the rail of the ship, and caught the sword as it fell, holding it up triumphantly.

Captain Trueblood, finally released from his rooted-to-the-spot state, gave a desperate high-pitched cry and leapt at HH, closely followed by Blackbeard.

They all arrived at exactly the same moment, and for a second I saw all three locked together in a kind of mad bundle with too many arms and legs. Then, just as quickly, they were gone. A loud splash followed, and everyone, prisoners and pirates alike, forgot they were enemies and rushed to the rail to look down.

All we could see was a spreading circle of ripples where the two men and Henry Hunter had hit the water.

MYSTERIES
OF THE DEEP

I don't know how long I stood there, watching
the ripples vanish as the surface of the water
returned to flat calm. No one said anything.
Half of me wanted to jump in after them,
but the sensible half reminded me that I was
not a great swimmer and that there could be
sharks... I knew Henry was a strong swimmer
and so I waited, expecting to see his head

break the surface at any moment.

When it didn't and the seconds dragged on into minutes, I began to feel like every bit of me had turned to lead. There was no way I could believe Henry had gone, that I might never see him again. Henry always had a solution for any situation and this time could not possibly be different.

And as it happened I had other things to think about anyway. Everyone on *Destiny's Wyrd* had.

Because, as you will have probably worked out, as soon as the Sword of Columbus vanished into the sea, everything the object had been holding together began to disintegrate. Both the cursed pirates – and the ship.

The first to go were the crew. I turned to see Caraway literally dissolving. He had a surprised look on his face – his face being the last thing to disappear as the rest of him slowly faded away. I caught sight of Cyrus Firestone, with a triumphant grin on his face, putting his fist right through Pockmark as he too simply melted away. Jake, who had recovered from Blackbeard's blow, tried to swing his iron fist at another man and it went right though him.

One by one, the pirates vanished before our eyes.

Within minutes of the sword going over the side the entire crew had disappeared. I suddenly panicked. Surely the ship would follow suit. I looked up and saw the sails beginning to dissolve, followed by the masts. The deck itself began to feel strangely spongy under my feet and in places I could see right through it.

"Quick!" I shouted as loudly as I could to my fellow prisoners – although of course we were prisoners no more. "The ship is dissolving. We need to get to the *Spinnaker*!"

People began running in every direction at once, falling over each other, yelling and screaming. At least they seemed a lot less dazed now – I guessed because the curse had been lifted. A couple of people tried to grab hold of bits of the ship, only to find themselves clutching nothing but thin air as the timbers turned to dust.

I couldn't get to the *Spinnaker* in time. I felt the cold knife of the water as I fell into the ocean, and began paddling about desperately. I couldn't keep this up for long – I could just about doggy paddle, but as I've said before, I'm really not a great swimmer.

As the last of us fell into the water, *Destiny's Wyrd* faded out of existence. But I couldn't even feel relief. I was in the middle of the ocean, and numb at the loss of Henry Hunter.

The crew of the *Spinnaker*, who seemed to have been hiding below deck (who could blame them?), suddenly appeared on board the yacht. Seeing what was going on, they began to throw lifebelts down to us. I managed to grab one and waited as they lowered a small boat down and started hauling people on board as fast as they could.

Soon we were all aboard the yacht, being wrapped in blankets and offered mugs of steaming hot cocoa.

The shock of being plunged into the sea and then rescued had removed any last traces of whatever it was that had kept the prisoners dazed and confused. All around me they were demanding to know what was going on and where they were. All I could do was cling to the rail of the deck and stare down into the sea at the spot where Henry Hunter, Blackbeard and Captain Trueblood had vanished.

I knew that no human being could hold his or her breath this long. Not even Henry

Hunter. Somehow I had to come to terms with the fact that my best friend was not coming back – that I would never see him again.

I was about to turn sadly away when I noticed a long trail of bubbles rising to the surface of the sea.

What happened next is as about as weird as anything I've ever experienced in my adventures with Henry Hunter. In fact, it's so strange that among those on the *Spinnaker* who happened to be looking overboard there are two very different versions. One is what the recently released prisoners from the ghost ship, and the crew of the *Spinnaker* claimed they saw, the other is what yours truly, Dolf Pringle, will always believe I saw.

Some people say that what surfaced was an elaborately carved ship's dinghy, which had probably been sitting on the bed of the sea for a while, and that all the kerfuffle with the ghost ship and people falling overboard had somehow freed it.

What *I* saw was this.

The stream of bubbles heralded the appearance of the strangest-looking vehicle I had ever seen. I say 'vehicle' because there really isn't a word for what emerged from the depths of the ocean. The nearest thing I can compare it to is a Roman chariot, like the ones they used in that famous race scene from the old classic movie *Ben Hur*. Except that this one looked as if it was made of fish bones – huge, white fish bones, carved with all kinds of fancy designs. It literally shot out on the water, hovered for a second, then splashed back down and settled on the surface.

But it wasn't that which took my breath away. It was the sight of Henry Hunter standing in the middle of it!

Henry waved cheerfully to me and in moments he was climbing aboard the *Spinnaker*, as the chariot (or whatever it was) disappeared back into the ocean.

I have to admit that I rushed over to HH and hugged him like we hadn't seen each other in years. A bit embarrassing, I know, but there you are.

This of course meant the former prisoners and the *Spinnaker*'s crew began asking even more questions. Then I realised something. Captain Trueblood had not reappeared. I examined the ocean. No bubbles.

Henry saw me staring at the waves. He shook his head. "I don't think the Captain will be joining us, Dolf," he said. "I think he's found a new home – with Davy Jones."

Much like everyone around me I was bursting with questions – the most important being how Henry had survived his plunge into the ocean and what on earth was that thing he had been standing in. I looked back down over the side of the yacht and for a moment I thought I saw it again, drifting down to the seabed. I thought I saw something else, too: a face, framed by long green-gold hair, with big blue eyes that stared back at me. Then it was gone.

At this moment Iron Jake came over and clapped Henry on the back "Nice goin', boys," he said. Then, grinning at me, he added: "See – told yer mermaids were real!"

I had to wait a while before I could hear Henry's account of what happened after he fell overboard. I guessed he didn't want to tell everyone, so I didn't ask until we were alone. The rescued prisoners took a long time to settle down and the crew of the *Spinnaker* seemed not to know what to do without their captain. Finally the first mate, Thomas, who turned out to be a reasonable sort of bloke who admitted he had never been happy with what his boss was getting up to, took over as acting captain. He gave orders to the crew to make the prisoners comfortable for the night and the *Spinnaker* got under way.

Henry and I found a quiet corner in one of the swanky staterooms.

"So what happened?" I demanded.

Henry looked at me, his eyes deep and serious. "To be honest, I can't quite work it all out myself, but here's what I do know. As soon as we hit the water, Blackbeard began to melt away, just as we'd thought."

I nodded. "That's exactly what happened to the crew and the boat – they fell to pieces."

Henry looked as though he was going to ask me for a more detailed account, then he saw the look on my face and continued with his own tale.

"That left Trueblood with the sword. Not

that it did him much good, of course, as he kept sinking deeper into the sea. It looked like the sword was pulling him down, but he was too mad with greed to let go of it. I was tangled up with him too. I tried to get away, but Trueblood was dragging me down."

Henry paused.

"Er... well, to be honest, Dolf, I'm not sure what actually did happen next. I could say that I found myself able to breathe underwater and that... someone... came and picked me up... But everything gets a bit vague from then on."

Now if you knew Henry Hunter as well as I do you'd know that he's never this vague. And I mean *never*.

"So let me get this straight," I said, trying not to look too disbelieving. "You sank to the bottom of the sea and found you could breathe underwater and then someone came and... and what, exactly?"

"Well, if you'll believe me, I was taken by… some kind of sea people. They seemed to be waiting for me. And for Trueblood. He was looking dazed and pale, and they led him away, but put me into that chariot thing and sent me back up," Henry concluded.

I stared at him, wondering if the experience had sent him crazy.

Henry shrugged and then gave me his biggest grin. "Like I told you, Dolf," he said, flicking back the hair from his eyes, "you can't say something didn't happen or doesn't exist till you've seen it for yourself."

I thought of the face I had glimpsed in the water and shook my head. None of what Henry told me made any sense – unless you believe in sea people and mermaids and stuff, but sometimes things are just like that – especially when you hang around with Henry Hunter.

I still don't know what to believe. That day, Henry showed me a piece of carved bone. Narwhale's tusk, he said it was. I examined it, taking in the most amazingly detailed pictures engraved on its surface. "It's called scrimshaw work, Dolf. Old sailors used to spend their time carving this kind of thing when they had nothing else to do. I picked it up from the seabed."

I've got it here with me now. It's pretty worn, but the pictures seem to show a city of some kind, which is pretty obviously meant to be under the sea. There are some strange-looking people on it too, with long flowing hair and flipper-like legs, apparently swimming around, but I can't be sure if I'm really seeing them properly. Don't ask me what it means, or if Henry really did visit the sea people — and especially don't ask me if I saw a mermaid. I can't tell you.

Later on we spoke briefly about it with Iron Jake. When he heard Henry's version of what had happened he gave us both a strange look. "Tis easy enough told. You was taken by the Sea People. They knows a thing or two down below. They knew about them cursed pirates and their kind, and they were ready and waitin' for you as well. As to Cap'n Teach – I've no doubt he's entertainin' Davy Jones hi'self right now. I'm not sure about that nasty old Trueblood fella, but I'm sure we won't be seeing him again. And good riddance is what I say."

It took a while to sort out everything once we got back to port. The authorities had to be brought in, of course, but they seemed unconcerned by tales of cursed pirates and ghostly ships. All they were really interested in was that Captain Trueblood had broken the law in all kinds of ways by kidnapping people to help *him* look for treasure. That was clearly the only version of the story they were going to believe, but since there was no sign of Nathan Trueblood there was no one to prosecute. At least all the former prisoners could return home. That was all we'd ever wanted, anyway – to find Charlie's parents and bring them back home.

The crew of the *Spinnaker* were let off with fines since there was no real evidence that any of them had caused any physical harm to the captives and they had been following Captain Trueblood's orders. the *Spinnaker* was impounded and then sold to help pay compensation to those who had been captured. Most of them, in fact, seemed to have forgotten about what really happened and, thanks to a few helpful words from Iron Jake, were convinced that modern-day pirates had kidnapped them. It was probably best that way.

One more surprise was waiting for us when we docked at Bridgetown. For once it was a pleasant one. There, on the dock, was a large figure with a bandage wrapped around his head. It was Joe.

None of us could quite believe it – Jake least of all. He pounded the huge man on the back until I thought he would knock him into the sea again. We learned that the *Moby Dick* had actually survived its run-in with the monster wave and was even now sitting in dry dock awaiting repairs. Joe had managed to cling onto a rope as the old tug almost capsized, and despite being banged about a good deal (hence the bandage) he had climbed back on board the *Moby* and piloted her back most of the way home, finally being picked up by a passing cruise ship and towed back to harbour. I couldn't be sure what pleased

Iron Jake the most, the fact that his old friend was alive or that his ship had survived – but in any case he could not stop beaming at everyone. Henry made him smile even more hugely when he promised to pay for the repairs to the *Moby Dick*. As he said: "After all, you never did get any of that treasure, so it's the least we can do."

The old sailor looked really quite sad to see us go in the end, though he muttered something about "Finally getting a bit o' peace an' quiet in me old age." Then he winked his good eye at us and added, "But if you're ever in these parts again, don't forget to look me up."

Once we were safely back at the hotel we found that Charlie Stevens had flown out to Barbados to be reunited with his parents on receiving the news that they were alive and well. I imagined Cousin Jack, back home in England, must have been feeling a bit stupid, having given up looking for them far too easily. I think he'd meant well enough, not wanting to give Charlie hope where there might not be any. Of course Charlie was over the moon to have his parents back and couldn't stop thanking us.

Before we all went our separate ways Mr Stevens took us aside.

"You know I can't say thank you enough times, boys," he said. "It's been a pretty traumatic six months – but at least I finally know what it feels like to find pirate gold." I thought I saw a twinkle in his eyes as he shook our hands.

Which just goes to show – not *everyone* forgot what really happened.

That's pretty much all there is to say about the adventure of the cursed pirates. But there's one other thing that I haven't yet explained. You see, HH has gone missing. No one has seen him since he vanished on a normal morning in May. No note. No clue as to where he might have gone. His parents organised a huge international search, but it failed to turn up anything. And I'm worried. Really worried. Everyone has given up looking, it seems – apart from me. He's got to be out there somewhere – maybe he's been kidnapped without a ransom but I'm not going to give up on him, any more than he gave up on Charlie's parents.

I'm looking at the piece of carved Narwhal tusk that Henry brought back from the deep, lying on my desk. I can't help wondering if it has anything to tell me about where my friend is right now. Did you notice any clues in this story? Please tell me if you did, because I'm not going to stop looking till I find out what happened to him. I'll keep searching through the Henry Hunter Files until I get him back – there must be some clues in our adventures somewhere...

Author's Note & Acknowledgements

Every book seems to stack up a bigger and bigger heap of thanks to all those who helped and offered support. This story from the Henry Hunter Files is no exception. Huge thanks go, as always, to my three most faithful readers: my wife Caitlin, who kept saying 'Tell me more' and suggested a brilliant title change; our son Emrys, who advised on the kinds of things twelve-year-old boys might say; and Ari Berk, who cheerfully read the first draft and told me it was going in the right direction.

Thanks also to Dwina Murphy-Gibb for

letting me steal bits of The Prebendal (not to mention the dogs) for Charlie Stevens' home; and to my old mate Mark Ryan, whose own piratical exploits in the TV show *Black Sails* are already legendary. Nor can I fail to give a big cheer to Amanda Wood at Templar for giving me the chance to explore so many obsessions through the writing of the Henry Hunter books. My editors, Emma Goldhawk and Tilda Johnson, not to mention the amazing Catherine Coe, copy-editor extraordinaire, kept me firmly on track and suggested some crucial amendments. Finally, not for the first time, I want to acknowledge the inspiration of the *Pirates of the Caribbean* movies. A visit to the set of *On Stranger Tides* re-inspired me at a point when I needed it. Thanks to all – especially Mike Stenson – for a great day.

I had fun re-creating the bits of the Caribbean where most of the story takes place, though I occasionally played fast and loose with some of the locations in order to make them work. There really is a museum of piracy similar to the one described here, but it's on the wonderful island of Nassau, not Barbados. As far as I know there are no suspicious people hanging about there (though you never know), and it doesn't have a basement with skeletons. If you ever get a chance to go it's well worth a visit. Other than this all the facts about pirates that Henry talks about in the book are real. Blackbeard really lived, of course, and was every bit as nasty as described. His last command was not called *Destiny's Wyrd*, however, but the *Queen Ann's Revenge*. As to what happened to his treasure... that's another story.

John Matthews, Oxford, 2014